Mattie Celi

M. Elizabeth Schaefer

outskirtspress

DENVER, COLORADO

Outskirts Press, Inc.
http://www.outskirtspress.com

ISBN: 978-1-4787-6545-5

Outskirts Press and the "OP" logo are trademarks belonging to Outskirts Press, Inc.

PRINTED IN THE UNITED STATES OF AMERICA

This book is dedicated to
MARLEY LAURYN LEEDY

And
In Memoriam
Luna Elizabeth Leedy
12/3/2014 – 1/5/2015

Many thanks to my husband Marshall, my son Jess Leedy,
my brother Louis Fetherolf, and my treasured friend Kim Cross,
for their encouragement and support in writing this story.

CHAPTER ONE

January 2006 – Simi Valley, California

My brothers, sister and I ate our lone serving of mashed potatoes without a word. Our stepfather, the old man, was drunk again.

"Where's the butter, woman!" the old man yelled, as he shoved his plate filled with steak, potatoes and broccoli, aside.

I forced another forkful into my mouth and tried to swallow. I wanted to shove more than mashed potatoes down *his* throat, but he was 6 feet 3 inches tall, and I was only 4 foot 11 and fourteen years old. I referred to him as the "old man" because I didn't think he deserved a name. His white hair, muscular body, and mean face scared and intimidated people. Even when he wasn't drinking, he was mean.

He said his hair turned white when he was seventeen years old. I figured it must have been something really traumatic that happened to him. He would never say. He *always* seemed stressed or angry.

"We're all out, I forgot..." my mother began.

I cupped my hands in my lap and tried to stop them from shaking. My older brother Louis put one hand over mine and squeezed lightly. I briefly looked over at my younger sister, Angie. She had a tear running down her cheek.

My heart sank into an abyss. My younger brothers, Tony and Matt froze like statues glaring at me and Louis. Their eyes turning dark with fear and pain made my stomach clench so tight it hurt. I wanted to put my arms around them and tell them everything was going to be okay, but I didn't dare move.

"Can't you do anything right, woman?" WHACK! The old man smacked my mother hard across the face. Her head hit the wall, and she slumped to the floor. I gasped. Louis jumped to his feet. "Louis, no!" I whispered. He helped Mom back into her chair.

"Get the hell out of here, NOW! GET OUT!" the old man screamed at Louis.

Angie, Tony, and Matt ran to their bedrooms. I ran out the front door behind Louis and over to our neighbor's house for help - again.

"Do you want to call the police, Mattie, Louis?" Mrs. Outen asked.

"No," I replied. "I'm sure my mom would lie again and tell the police she tripped and fell - or something. The old man would be super nice to the police. The last time the police came to the house, I heard the old man tell them, "These unruly kids don't appreciate the roof I've put over their heads or the food I put in their mouths."

"Food? Right! We kids are nearly starving," Louis said. "I wanted to deck him. I tried that before, but it only made things worse. Mom won't press charges. It's hopeless."

Louis had decked the old man once before when he choked our mom. When the old man came to, he went to the kitchen and returned with a huge knife…well, it wasn't a fun evening. He held the knife up to Louis' throat and then mine. I couldn't speak for fear it would cut me. Louis had to do a lot of talking to get the old man to put the knife down. Mom sat there with her head down, staring at her cupped hands in her lap.

I was shaking and wringing my hands as I told Mrs. Outen,

"The old man hit my mom across the face. Her head hit the wall, and she fell to the floor leaving a trail of blood on the wall. When Louis helped her back into the chair, the old man screamed at him to get out and I followed him."

Mom had been acting more strange ever since Angie and I told her that the old man was coming into our room at night, drunk, touching my breasts and saying weird things to me like, "Would you have anything to do with me if something happened to your mother?" I would pull the covers up to my neck and curl into a fetal position. I nearly vomited when he breathed on me. It freaked me out. Angie pretended to be asleep.

Then he would get mad, and leave the room cussing and slamming the door.

"That's it," Mrs. Outen said as she took a long, deep breath and shook her head. "We have to do something. You two must leave your house for a while before someone ends up in the hospital or worse. Louis, I suggest you go stay with Ken and his family for a while if you can. I have a plan for Mattie. She will tell your mother where you're going."

Louis called his best friend Ken. Ken and his father came right away to pick him up. Louis and I hugged each other.

"I'll see you soon," Louis said.

I stopped myself from tearing up. I watched Louis' face in the car as he waved to me while the car pulled away. I tried to smile as I waved back at him.

Mrs. Outen made me a cup of tea. We sat and talked for a while and then she said, "Mattie dear, you must go to your school counselor tomorrow right after school and tell her you don't want to go home. Mrs. Henson, right?"

I nodded.

"Tell her why you are afraid to go home. Tell her what has been going on at your house. She'll take it from there. This madness has to stop."

"What will happen to me?" I asked - my stomach cramping. "And, what will happen to Angie and the boys, after I leave?"

"Mrs. Henson will call Child Protective Services (CPS). They will send someone to the school to talk to you. They will take care of you, Mattie. Hopefully, once your mother and stepfather are notified by the authorities that you are not coming home, things will calm down for a bit. Now, you must go home. Hopefully, things have quieted down at your house. Put some of your things in this tote bag to take with you tomorrow. Be strong. I'll be in touch."

I was relieved to find the old man had passed out when I returned to the house. I didn't call it "home." It was more like a creepy mental institution. And Mom was fading away little by little. The house was a depressing mish-mash of cheap furniture. A picture of a meadow in winter hung crookedly on the living room wall. No one bothered to straighten it up because it would go crooked again when the old man slammed the front door or hit the wall with his fist. Mom was holding an ice pack to her face and motioned for me to go to bed.

I whispered, "Louis went to stay at Ken's house."

She nodded.

I couldn't go to sleep. I could hear my heart pounding in the silence. It hurt a little, too. I wondered if I was having a heart attack. I hoped the old man would stay passed out all night. Angie woke up and snuggled next to me.

"Everything's going to be okay," I whispered in her ear.

If the old man so much as yells at Angie when I'm gone, I'll... I wish Mom would hit that creepy raging, angry, stupid, alcoholic bully with a baseball bat and end it right there. I'm tired of him beating on us and making us go hungry while he eats steak. He says he needs his strength to work. No, he needs his strength to beat on us. I hate him, and I hate my mother for letting him abuse us.

I knew I was going to miss my sweet little sister and brothers so much, but I also knew Mrs. Outen was right. I *had* to leave to make it better for the other kids. I hoped it wouldn't make it worse, and that Mom would wake up to the reality of the situation when she realized I was gone and not coming back.

Mom used to be pretty with her dark curly hair and strong fingernails. She would put a fingernail under my chin and push up and up until I was on my tippy-toes and tell me, "You'd better listen to me young lady, you hear me?"

"Yes," I would quickly reply, hoping her nail wouldn't be stuck in my chin forever, and I could put my feet back down on the ground! Now she looked thin and gaunt, with dark circles under her eyes.

I thought about our neighbor, Mrs. Outen. She was so cool. She was a large woman who looked like a huge balloon when she wore those big, colorful Hawaiian Mumu's. She would read ten to fifteen books a week! I got interested in reading one day when she told me, "Honey, reading takes you into another world. You forget all about the 'here and now.' It's wonderful!"

Mr. and Mrs. Outen were intellectuals. Mr. Outen was a Nuclear Scientist. He was very nice, but wasn't much of a people person. He explained their relationship by saying, "My "Wifey-weed" runs the front office, and I take care of business from the back room." Whatever that means... I guess I'll understand when I get older.

Louis and I took turns babysitting their two little adopted boys. Mrs. Outen also gave me extra money for cleaning her house. The old man took the money out of our hands as soon as we walked through the front door. Sometimes Mrs. Outen would stick a five dollar bill in our pockets and tell us to use it to buy a hot lunch at school. I would buy food to sneak home for Angie and my brothers, ever since Tony told me he stole some candy bars at the drug store for him and Matt. I told him not to *ever* do that again. I knew why they were hungry. The old man had put them in their bedroom for an entire weekend with just bread and water for punishment. The jerk did that often.

He had my two little brothers dig a hole in the back yard for a swimming pool that he never planned to put in. The old man caught them taking a break in the shade and drinking water from the garden hose. It was summer and hot in the sun. He beat both of them with a belt and told them they would take breaks when he told them to. He told my mom that it would keep them off the street and out of trouble.

The next day after school, I walked to Mrs. Henson's office and stood inside the door. Mrs. Henson saw me and waved me in to sit in the chair in front of her desk while she finished her phone conversation.

Mrs. Henson wore an old-fashioned navy and white printed dress with small, gold hoop earrings. Her hair was light brown, medium length, and combed back in soft waves. I looked around the office. It looked cozy. Light green curtains with muted leaves on them covered the one window. A crystal candy jar and other little knick-knacks that people had given her were strategically placed on her desk. I could tell she loved every one of them.

I lifted the edge of a doily on the corner of the desk and noticed the lace pattern of dust underneath it. I calmed down a little. I liked Mrs. Henson and hoped that she would help me.

Mrs. Henson ended her phone conversation and turned her attention to me.

"Well, Mattie, what can I do for you?"

"Mrs. Henson," I cleared my throat. "I don't want to go home."

Mrs. Henson's smile turned to concern.

"Why don't you want to go home, Mattie?"

I told Mrs. Henson what happened the night before about how

the old man had been beating my mom, us kids, and making us almost starve while he ate big meals in front of us. When I got to the part about the old man coming in to my room at night, touching my breasts and saying weird things to me, Mrs. Henson put her palm up in the air and said, "Mattie, stop."

She leaned forward over her desk, with her hands pressed together, and looked straight into my eyes.

"I'm surprised...no, I'm shocked! Mattie, are you absolutely telling me the truth? I sure don't want to believe this," she said as she got up and closed her office door.

"Yes, it is true and I'm scared."

I started to cry. Mrs. Henson handed me some tissue.

"Is the old man your stepfather?"

"Yes. We call him the old man because we don't think he deserves a real name."

Mrs. Henson put her hand on the phone and then looked at me for a moment.

"Mattie, I'm going to call Social Services in Ventura and have someone come out to hear your story. Is that okay with you?"

"Yes," I said in a quivering voice. My hands were cold, so I put them under my armpits to get them warm.

While Mrs. Henson was on the phone, I wondered if I should really be doing this. Would it make the old man get more violent when he found out where I was and why?

And, my mom...I hoped she wouldn't totally lose it.

Mrs. Henson got off the phone and was saying something to me, but all I heard was a hollow mumbling sound, like she was talking from inside a tunnel. It was weird. I nodded my head up and down as she talked.

Mrs. Astor from Social Services arrived a few minutes later. She wore a black pencil skirt and a blue, pastel sweater. Her hair was short and spikey. I liked her immediately.

"Hi, Mattie, I'm Mrs. Astor. I understand you don't want to go home. Will you tell me why?"

I spent the next few minutes telling Mrs. Astor the same things I told Mrs. Henson, and a little more about how Mrs. Outen had helped me and Louis.

I ended with, "I'm worried about my sister and brothers."

"What are their names and ages, Mattie?"

"Angie is 10, Tony is 8, and Matt is 6. My brother Louis is 16. He'll be 17 in May. He went to stay at his friend's house for a while."

"Mattie, I'm going to take you to Juvenile Hall in Ventura. There are two areas; one side is where the delinquents stay and the other area is the dependent side. You'll stay in the dependent area while we get things straightened out. Is this okay with you?"

I nodded.

When Mrs. Astor hugged Mrs. Henson, I felt better that they were friends. I thanked Mrs. Henson. Mrs. Astor drove me to Juvenile Hall. On the way, we talked about the abuse at my house. My stomach was growling out loud. I was hungry. But then, I was used to being hungry.

It was dark and cold outside. I looked up at the moon as it went behind some creepy, dark clouds, came back out and then back behind again. I wondered what Juvenile Hall was going to be like. I was tired and scared.

Chapter 2

Mrs. Astor checked me into Juvenile Hall. She told me I would
have to have a physical examination by the staff doctor.

"Mattie, this is Dr. Wood. He will take you through a health
screening process which will include an examination for possible
sexual abuse. I'll be in the waiting room. I'll see you when you're
done," said Mrs. Astor.

Dr. Wood examined me from head to toe. The nurse held my
hand and stayed next to me. It was as though she understood how
scared I was and wanted to comfort me. It helped. I felt my face turn
red when Dr. Wood examined my breasts. I almost pulled the sheet
up to my chin. How could he like doing this kind of stuff? It was
embarrassing and annoying.

"Miss Celi, I am now going to look at your upper body for any
unusual marks."

He sounded like a robot. The doctor told me what he was going
to do before he did it. The nurse guided me through the most hu-
miliating part, the sexual abuse examination, by explaining the process and holding my hand. I wanted to kick him. The doctor never
looked at me. He just kept writing stuff down on a chart. Then he
told the nurse to bring in Mrs. Astor.

"She looks to be in good health. There is no evidence of sexual
abuse. She is a virgin."

I could've told the doctor that if he'd just asked me. I thought this must be what a lab rat feels like. I got dressed so fast it must've looked like a silent movie in high speed.

Mrs. Astor and I headed down a hallway and ran into Ms. Middle.

"Mattie, this is Ms. Middle. She is a Juvenile Detention Officer or "JDO" as we call them. She will take you to the dependent area and get you settled. In a couple of days you'll have a hearing in court. A judge will hear your case and decide whether to send you back home or to place you in foster care."

"What if they send me back home? Will my mom be in court with me?" I asked.

"Your mother and stepfather should be in court. I will be there with you."

"What will happen to my sister and brothers? Does my mom know where I am?"

I felt light headed and leaned back against the wall. I had a lot more questions to ask, but I couldn't think clearly.

"We'll take one thing at a time, Mattie. Yes, your mom knows you're here. Now, go with Ms. Middle and I'll see you in a day or so. Here is my card. If you need to talk to me, leave a message at this number and I'll get in touch with you, okay? Keep your chin up!"

Ms. Middle wore a dark blue uniform with her name and the letters "JDO" patched on her shirt pocket. She smiled at me and took me to the dependent side of Juvenile Hall. She walked me into the cell. It smelled musty and like bleach at the same time. I carefully placed my tote bag with my belongings on the hard gray mattress. I glanced at the toilet, the sink, and the bars on the small window above the bed.

"I thought I wasn't in trouble."

"You're not, Mattie," said Ms. Middle. "This wing is also used for overflow. All the cells…er, rooms…look the same."

I looked at the see-through iron door and then down at the lock. "Don't worry; I'll keep the door open for you."

My stomach flipped at the idea of sleeping here, all night. And, what about my...personal business? I glanced again at the toilet, with no stall, no curtain, nothing.

I shivered. I shouldn't be here. I wished I could take it all back and go home. At least I would be with Angie, Tony and Matt. Mom is probably going crazy. I was like her right arm. She taught me how to cook, clean, sew, and how to take care of my little brothers and sister. The old man better not take it out on her or the kids, or...

Ms. Middle was holding a tray of food.

"Is this for me?"

"Yes. I knew it would be late by the time you got here. Go ahead, eat!"

I couldn't believe it. A whole tray of food! I took a few bites and then put the fork down; I placed my hands in my lap and I started to cry.

"It's going to be okay, Mattie," said Ms. Middle. "You've probably been through a lot."

"I wish I could give some of this food to my sister and brothers." I was no longer hungry.

I woke up about midnight to use the toilet. Half asleep, I wondered where I was. As I sat on the toilet, I looked straight ahead through the iron door. It was locked. It was not supposed to be locked. I saw another woman JDO sitting at the table outside my cell. She looked at me and then back down at her book. At least I didn't have to worry about the old man coming in to bother me. I bit my bottom lip thinking about it. I hoped school tomorrow with the delinquent kids was going to be okay.

The next morning I was escorted to day school in Juvenile Hall by the daytime JDO, Ms. Turner. She wasn't real friendly, but she wasn't mean or cold. She was tall and slender with shoulder length auburn hair that turned under at the ends. Her skin was fair and freckled. The JDO working from midnight through to morning, Ms. Penny, didn't like me. I didn't like her either. She treated me like a delinquent and locked me in my cell at night. She had a short, square body, a square face and a square personality. Her short brown hair looked like a man's cut. She wore no makeup or jewelry. This morning before going to class she said, "Let's get moving little miss goody pants. You're not foolin' me, girl."

What the heck does that mean? She doesn't even know me.

I looked forward to seeing Ms. Middle when she came in the evenings. She talked to me like I was a good human being. One night she pulled out some materials and a box with sewing stuff in it. She was making her daughter's weird-sized doll some clothes – sewing them by hand. I told her I could sew and asked if I could help.

"Really, you can sew? Well, here's a skirt I cut out. Let's see what you can do."

I sewed the skirt together, put the snap set on the waistband in the back, hemmed the skirt, and handed it to her. She examined it inside and out. Her eyes got big.

"Wow, Mattie. Who taught you how to sew like this?"

"My mom taught me. We would mend the family's clothes."

From that night on, Ms. Middle let me sew with her. She even let me design some clothes for the doll. I never thought I could have so much fun sewing!

I was the only kid from the dependent side in class. I received a full set of stares and silence when I entered the classroom. A masculine-looking female instructor motioned for me to sit in a chair in the middle of the room.

"Hey, pretty girl. What are you doing here?" yelled one of the delinquent girls as the rest of the class laughed.

I turned and glared at the girl. I could tell my glare surprised her. The instructor told the girls to shut up and began roll call. When my name was called, the girls taunted me again by saying, "What a sweet, pretty girl you are, Mattie Celi."

Two male guards came into the room and stood in front of the class. When the instructor had to leave the room for a minute, four of the delinquent girls got into a fight after one girl ripped a porcelain nail off another girl's finger. The girl screamed when blood spurted out of her fingernail. She lunged at the girl that attacked her by pulling her hair and cussing her out. The other two girls jumped into the fight. They were punching and scratching the injured girl. The guards ran over and pulled the girls apart.

One guard took the injured girl out of the room as she kicked and screamed, "I'll get you, bitches. This isn't over. You better watch your backs, bitches!"

Two more guards came in. They grabbed and handcuffed the other three girls to desks in the back of the classroom. They told the girls to shut up. Most of the delinquent girls I saw had tattoos, nose, lip and earring holes, dark, dyed stringy hair, and long painted porcelain nails. They had to remove all rings and jewelry when they checked in to Juvenile Hall or "Juvy" as the kids called it. I had none of those things. My hair was straight and down past my shoulders, coffee brown in color, with long bangs that I combed to one side. I wore no makeup other than a little tinted lip gloss. My nails were natural and cut short. I was definitely different in their eyes. I could tell they were interested in me. I wasn't interested in them.

Later, we were all escorted into a mess hall for lunch. I marched through the line to get my food and kept my head up, scanning the tables for a place to sit - by myself. Two girls walked by me hissing as they scratched me on my arm. One of the scratches drew blood. They moved away fast and laughed. I stood up and glared at the girls as they methodically, one-by-one, sat down across from me. I ate the rest of my lunch staring at them and not flinching one bit. They didn't move. In a way, I sort of felt sorry for them. I figured they probably had as bad a childhood as I did, or maybe they were being brought up by tough-talking, druggy, street-gang type parents or relatives. Who knew? I refused to be a punk.

The next day during lunch, one of the girls named Marselda came at me with her nails to scratch my face. I ducked and pushed her right hand away with my left arm.

"Leave me alone," I told her in a strong, low voice. She swung at my face again.

I pushed her hand away, lunged out with my right hand and grabbed her throat. I squeezed hard enough to make her almost pass out. She fell to her knees, gasping and trying to catch her breath. The room got quiet. As I leaned down to help her up, I looked over at the guards. They looked away! I was amazed. Marselda walked away holding her throat, coughing, and looking back at me in surprise. The girls never bothered me after that. A few of the girls tried to befriend me, but I asked them to please leave me alone. And they did.

Two days later, Mrs. Astor came to visit me after class and before dinner. I told her what happened during class and lunch hour.

"I know. One of the guards told me. Mattie, try to stay away from those kids. You were fortunate the guards let you off. It may not happen next time. Where did you learn the self-defense technique you used on Marselda? Have you had any martial arts training?"

"No. My brother Louis taught me some street moves to keep bullies away."

"*Please* be careful, Mattie. Some of these kids have done brutal things to others, including murder."

My temples throbbed as she was talking to me about what could've happened. I developed an instant headache and my heart started racing. "I'm sorry. I will. They haven't bothered me since the incident."

Mrs. Astor put her hand to her face and shook her head. She was silent for a moment. I could tell she was shocked at what I had done. Then, out of nowhere, she asked, "Mattie, you told Ms. Middle you've been having a recurring dream about your stepfather. Can you tell me about it?"

"I guess. But I really want to forget it."

"No pressure, Mattie. It's up to you."

Mrs. Astor had been so good to me; I didn't want to disappoint her.

"I hear my mom crying. I walk down the hall to my mom and stepfather's bedroom. I turn the door knob and walk into the room. It's dark and quiet. I follow the edge of the bed with my left hand and walk around to the side where the old man is sleeping. There's a dim light shining down on his face. His eyes are closed. I raise my right hand in the air over his chest. In my hand is a huge knife. It's the same knife he had held to my throat the night he was choking my mom. I'm thinking the knife must come down fast and quick into his heart, so I can watch him take his last breath. Then his eyes open and he grabs my arm. I try to scream, but nothing comes out. I wake up and my heart is beating so hard it feels like it's going to pop out of my chest."

Mrs. Astor asked, "Do you really want to kill your stepfather, Mattie?"

Her question upset me. "Huh? No, of course not, but I wish he would go away forever."

I had a hard time going to sleep that night. I tossed and turned. I was so worried about going to court the next day. I woke up about 1:00AM and went to use the "totally out there in the open" toilet. Ms. Penny glared at me through the bars.

The next morning after breakfast, Mrs. Astor led me into the courtroom. We took our seats. My stomach felt like it had a brick in it. I looked across the room and saw my mom and the old man. I took a double take at the old man. He was wearing a new navy suit with a white shirt and yellow printed tie. His hair was neatly cut. I had never seen him dressed up. I soon realized it was to impress the Judge. He looked regal in that suit. My mother's eyes were glassy and she wasn't wearing lipstick. She *always* wore lipstick out in public. She looked tired and had black circles under her eyes. She was wearing a plain house dress. I couldn't tell if she was really looking at me. It was strange. I felt a deep sense of gloom.

I almost jumped out of my seat when the officer yelled, "All rise!"

The officer introduced the Judge. When the Judge sat down, the officer said, "Please be seated."

The Judge was an older man with short gray hair, bushy eyebrows and little beady eyes that made him look mean. He shuffled through the papers in front of him like he was sick of doing his job. Then he lowered his glasses on his nose, looked around, and proceeded to ask the old man some questions.

"Mr. O'Doherty, are these allegations of physical and sexual abuse true?"

The old man looked straight at the Judge and very calmly replied, "No, your Honor. They are not true." He then proceeded to tell the Judge how difficult it was to provide for my mom and *her* children.

The hearing didn't go well. My heart sank as the judge asked my mom, "Mrs. O'Doherty, do you believe your daughter's allegations are true?"

She paused for a second, and then replied, "No, your Honor," and then lowered her head.

I was in shock. My own Mother lied in court! I stared at her. She never raised her head again.

The Judge never asked *me* any questions. He lowered his head and looked over his glasses at me and said, "Miss Celi, after review-ing the health screening information by Dr. Wood, there is incon-clusive evidence of any abuse. Young lady, I am ordering you back to your home. I expect you to stop the attention-seeking behavior. Do you understand, Miss Celi?"

I was stunned. The Judge repeated himself with a little anger in his voice.

"Yes, sir," I replied, while the whole courtroom of people stared at me. At that moment, I felt like the world had walked away from me. I was numb. Mrs. Astor put her arm around me. I couldn't talk. She took me back to my cell. I sat on my cell bed while Mrs. Astor told Ms. Turner what happened. Ms. Turner looked surprised. I got up and gathered my things.

"Please tell Ms. Middle goodbye for me when she comes in. Goodbye, Ms. Turner."

"I will, Mattie. I'm so sorry. Good luck to you," she replied.

Mrs. Astor drove me back to the house. On the way, I thought about why I didn't speak until I was five years-old. Silence kept me somewhat safe. My real father was a physically abusive alcoholic. We lived in Chicago government housing. My mom went on Public Assistance and Food Stamps for a few years after she chased my fa-ther out the door with a heavy frying pan. She told him not to come back, ever. She had his belongings in trash bags and threw them out the door after him. He never came back. Fortunately, I began talk-ing a few days before I started Kindergarten. Mom said I haven't stopped talking since.

One day, a painter came to our two-story townhome in the proj-ects. I turned to go up the stairs after school. There was a tall man painting the wall. He said hello to me. I remember moving up the stairs away from him as fast as I could. He gave me the creeps then, and he gives me the creeps, now. He wooed Mom for weeks until she finally agreed to go out with him. Louis and I tried to tell her that he was nasty to us when she *wasn't* around and nice when she *was* around. She thought we were jealous of him. Now, she is married to the *old man;* another alcoholic abuser.

He moved us from Chicago out to California into a four bedroom house. We all slept on the floor until our furniture arrived. He started work right away; however, he lost several jobs because of his temper. He didn't like being told what to do. He told his bosses where to stick it. Now, he couldn't find work and he was taking it out on my family.

When we pulled in the driveway, I was shaking. I wanted to jump out of the car and run. My hands were sweaty and I kept licking my lips. Mrs. Astor walked with me up to the front door and rang the bell.

Chapter 3

"Hello, Mrs. Doherty," Mrs. Astor said.

"Hi, Mom."

"Mattie! Come in. Mrs. Astor, thank you for bringing Mattie home."

"You're welcome. I'll be on my way. Goodbye, Mattie," Mrs. Astor said as she handed Mom her card.

I was still shaking as I entered the house. I looked around and didn't see anyone.

"Sit here with me, Mattie. I'll fix us a cup of tea."

The garage door was closed when I arrived, so I wasn't sure if the old man was home. I watched Mom as she moved through the kitchen. Then I heard the *footsteps* coming down the hall. I froze. My heart started pounding. Mom brought a cup of tea over to me. When she put the cup down, it clattered and some of the tea spilled into the saucer. She was definitely nervous. The old man walked into the kitchen. As soon as he looked at me, he lost it.

"Who the hell do you think you are, you little bitch? You think you can waltz back in this house and..."

Mom picked up the hot tea pot and moved toward him screaming, "STOP IT! I've had enough. Enough is enough!"

The old man moved toward Mom and raised his arm to strike her.

"I mean it! I'll burn your eyes out with this boiling water. I MEAN IT!" Mom cried.

He looked at her in surprise and put his arm down. I was so glad to see my mom defend us. But, I was also frightened that he would get more violent. I stood up and looked right at him. He wouldn't look at me. He continued spewing obscenities as he moved past Mom. The whole house shook when he slammed the door to the garage. A minute later, we heard tires screeching down the street. I hoped something would happen so he would never return to our lives. He was evil.

"Mom, maybe I shouldn't stay here. Maybe we should call Mrs. Astor. I don't want anyone to get hurt."

Mom was shaking. I went over to her and hugged her. She didn't respond. She sat down and said, matter-of-factly, "Let's have our tea and calm down. He's not going to hurt anyone."

There was so much I wanted to say to her. I wanted to comfort her and tell her she could get rid of him. Louis and I would take care of her and the kids. I wanted to convince her to put him behind bars for a long time. I wanted to ask her why she chose him over us kids and allowed him to abuse us. It was getting worse, much worse. I knew I was only fourteen, but I also knew what was happening to my mom and it hurt.

Angie, Tony and Matt came in through the front door from school. They ran over and hugged me.

"Are you home to stay, Mattie?" asked Angie.

"Yes, I missed you guys." I hugged all three of them. I was so happy to see them that I forgot what had just happened. While they went to their rooms to change clothes, I turned to see how Mom was doing.

"Mom, have you seen or talked to Louis?"

"Yes, he's still at Ken's house. He said he will come to see us soon."

That evening, I was standing at the kitchen sink peeling potatoes like I always had, when the old man came in the kitchen to throw something in the trash. He leaned down and picked up a handful of peelings out of the trash, threw them on the counter in front of me, and began to yell at me.

"What the hell are you doing wasting so much potato. You're supposed to peel the skin off, not the whole damned potato. Look at me when I'm talking to you!"

I looked at him. He stepped back and kicked me real hard in the back of my left thigh with his steel-toed work boot. I yelled and fell to the floor. He hit me so hard that my knee hit the cupboard handle. It was bleeding and swelling fast.

"Get up! Go to your room, you little bitch, NOW!"

He was about to kick me in the head when Mom threatened him.

"That's it, I'm calling the police!" Mom yelled as she moved for the phone.

The old man yanked the phone cord out of the wall and said, "You're not calling anyone."

He opened a cupboard, grabbed a bottle of booze, slammed the cupboard shut and stormed off to his bedroom. Mom helped me into a chair and cleaned up my knee. Angie helped me to our bedroom. The boys had already gone to their room. I sat down on the bed with Angie and held her hand. We ate no dinner that night.

"Angie, what did you tell the investigator that came here about what happened?"

Angie's eyes got big. "Nothing, no one asked me anything. The lady only talked to Mom and the old man. Mom made us go to our rooms. I couldn't hear what they were saying."

I had asked Mrs. Astor to have someone talk to my sister. I knew Angie would tell the truth about what happened.

Mom came in with a cold pack for my bruised thigh. I tried to talk to her, but she put her finger up to her lips and shook her head back and forth. I wondered what it would take to make her leave the old man before someone got seriously hurt or even killed. Louis and I had told her many times that we were willing to get jobs. I could babysit and Louis said he could get a job at the bowling alley after school. But she wouldn't go for it.

I waited until Angie fell asleep and proceeded to fill my tote bag - again.

The next morning, I went straight to Mrs. Henson's office before school started.

"Come in and sit down, Mattie. You're limping, is everything okay?"

"No. The old man kicked me last night in my thigh with his work boot. It really hurts. Do you want to see it?"

"Oh dear, yes, but let me close my door and the curtains first."

I lifted my skirt and she gasped, "Oh no, Mattie. What happened? That is the biggest, ugliest bruise I've ever seen. Why, it's the size of a football. I'm so sorry. Have a seat, Mattie. I'll call Mrs. Astor." She reached for the phone shaking her head.

I decided to remain standing. It hurt to sit down and it hurt to stand. My leg had swollen quite a bit from the night before and was turning an ugly dark purple and my knee had swollen more as well. My whole leg hurt. Mrs. Henson got me a cold pack to put under my thigh so I could sit down. She told me I could take it with me.

Mrs. Astor came right away to pick me up. I showed her my bruised thigh and my knee. She made a puckered face.

"Oh boy, that looks horrible. I'm so sorry, Mattie."

I told her what happened as we drove back to Juvenile Hall.

"Did you say anything to your stepfather that would make him mad enough to kick you?"

"No. He told me to look at him when he talked to me and when I did, he kicked me. If I had back-talked, he would've beaten the crap out of me!"

That evening while I was in my cell, Ms. Middle told me that she heard the old man had been arrested and then released on bail. Mom had told the police she didn't see him kick me. A police officer came to take pictures of my injuries. Ms. Middle was standing behind the policewoman as she took the pictures and mumbled, "Oh my God, Mattie."

I was taken to see Dr. Wood that afternoon after the pictures were taken. Doctor Wood didn't say a word. He gave me some Ibuprophen to take and some sports pain cream to put on the bruise. When I sat down, I had to lean on my right butt. It must've looked strange.

I had a hard time getting to sleep that night. My leg hurt. The Ibuprophen didn't kill the pain. When I finally dropped off to sleep, I had my recurring dream. I woke up the next morning sweaty and my teeth were sore from grinding them all night. I lay there getting angrier about the old man and my mother. I cried quietly thinking about how my mom had lied about what happened. She had abandoned me. And for the *old man!* How could she let him abuse her and us kids? What was wrong with her? I wished I could take Angie, Tony and Matt away from her. *No one* would believe me about the old man until he left proof on my leg! What's up with that?

I had been back in Juvenile Hall a few days when Mrs. Astor came to tell me she received an order from the court to place me in foster care. Good, I thought, I don't have to go back to court.

She said, "I'll start looking right away, Mattie. It might take a while, though. Kids your age are hard to place in foster homes. You'll have to be patient, okay?"

"What about Mr. and Mrs. Outen?" I asked.

"I'm sorry, but your Mother had a "Restraining Order" put in place for the Outens. They cannot talk to you or see you while you are a ward of the court. Your Mother said, "'Mrs. Outen is trying to steal my daughter.'"

I stood there wringing my hands while she told me. I walked back and forth trying not to think hateful thoughts about my mother. It wasn't working. I didn't feel sorry for her anymore. She needed an intervention. Right, like that would really help. The old man *and* my mom are both wacked-out. The old man went to court and got a slap on the wrist. He's free again to abuse my family. I hate him and I hate my mother for letting him abuse us.

Two more weeks went by and the delinquent girls in class continued trying to befriend me. I knew they were curious about me, so I started talking to them just enough to let them know that I was just like them - an abused kid that hated my stepfather. They could relate, but I didn't hang with them. Marselda asked me to teach her some street moves.

"I can't do that, Marselda. I'm trying to stay out of trouble and that definitely wouldn't help. I'm sorry."

"I guess you're right. Thanks anyway." Marselda pouted with disappointment.

The first Sunday in February arrived. I was told I had visitors and was escorted to the visiting area. I was hoping it was Louis or even my mother. To my surprise, it was my math teacher from school and his wife.

"Mr. Sweet!"

"Hi, Mattie, this is my wife, Shirley."

"Hi. It's so nice to meet you. How did you guys know I was here?"

"I saw Louis yesterday. He said he's staying with Ken and his family. He told me where you were. He's so upset about what is happening. I was shocked when I found out. I'm so sorry you're going through this, Mattie. You don't deserve it. Shirley and I want to know if you would like to come and stay with us. We have an extra bedroom and you could ride to and from school with us," Mr. Sweet said. I could tell he was serious.

I looked at his wife. She had a pretty face, shoulder length blond hair, blue eyes and was wearing a red sweater and tan colored slacks. Her smile was warm and gentle. I was happy for Mr. Sweet. Mr. Sweet was tall, blond, and my overall favorite teacher.

Mrs. Sweet smiled, "We would love to have you come and live with us, Mattie. We have already started the process of becoming foster parents. What do you say?"

"Yes! I would love... Are you sure? I mean, are you really sure you want to be foster parents?" I stammered.

Mr. and Mrs. Sweet laughed. They hugged me before they left and said they would see me soon.

I was so surprised. This was so cool! I didn't know what to think. I thought I was doomed to stay in Juvy until I turned eighteen.

The night before I was to go to the Sweets, I was excited and couldn't sleep. I wondered what it was going to be like being a foster kid. I got up to use the toilet a couple of times and saw "Ms. "Grumpy Penny" looking at me through the bars and then back down at her book. I was glad she was there during the night and not during the day.

Mrs. Astor picked me up from Juvenile Hall and drove me to the Sweet's home on Friday evening. It was a beautiful home up in the hills of Newbury Park, California. I thanked Mrs. Astor for everything before she pushed the doorbell button. We were greeted at the front door by Mr. and Mrs. Sweet, their five-year old daughter, Traci, and three-year old son, Scotty.

"Hello there! Come on in," Mr. Sweet said with a big smile.

Mr. Sweet introduced Traci and Scotty to us. Mrs. Astor gave Mrs. Sweet her card.

"I'm sorry I have to leave so soon, but I have plans for this evening. Mattie, take care. You're obviously in good hands. I'll be in touch. Goodbye kids, have fun," Mrs. Astor looked happy for me and departed with a smile.

The Sweets had some hot cocoa and shortbread cookies wait-ing for us. Scotty and Traci sat beside me at the kitchen table, both studying me as we all talked.

Traci blurted out, "Mattie, wanna see where you're gonna sleep?"

"Yeah, we can show you, if you want," Scotty said as both kids jumped up and down while holding my hands. Traci and Scotty were adorable. They made me think of Angie, Tony and Matt. I hoped they were okay. I missed them terribly.

Mrs. Sweet said, "We'll show you your room and then give you a tour of the house, okay Mattie?"

"Yes, thank you," I replied, giggling along with the kids.

My new room was somewhat small and nicely decorated with a single bed, turquoise and white bedding, an oak nightstand and dresser set along with a nice closet. The carpet was light, neutral tweed. A small banner was attached to the lamp on the nightstand. It read, WELCOME MATTIE!!!! I was totally blown away. Traci and Scotty stayed on either side of me holding my hands as Mrs. Sweet showed me the rest of their beautiful home. I immediately felt comfortable.

The kids stayed next to me for the rest of the evening until they went to bed. The Sweets stayed up a while longer to chat with me. We discussed their schedules.

"You can ride to and from school with us," said Mrs. Sweet.

Mr. Sweet added, "I'll be teaching high school next year. You'll have to see Mrs. Henson about another math class. Since you're liv-ing with us, I cannot remain your math teacher."

"Okay, I understand."

While I lay in bed that night in my new room, I couldn't believe where I was and who I was with. The kids were so cute. I'll take good care of them for the Sweets. I kept thinking, am I in heaven? Are these people real? I can't wait to tell Mrs. Henson when I get to school Monday.

Chapter 4

I was happy to be back in school. I went to see Mrs. Henson. She told me how happy she was that I was living with the wonderful Sweet family. I showed her the bruise on my thigh. The swelling had gone down somewhat, and the color was now mustard yellow and blue. The soreness was not as bad, and my knee had healed up. I could finally sit in a chair without pain.

Mrs. Henson hooked me up with another math teacher, Mr. Edwards. It wouldn't be long before school was out; another three months. That September, I would start my freshman year in High School.

"Mrs. Henson, what do I tell kids when they ask where I've been for the last few weeks? I don't want anyone to know my personal business, I mean, that I'm a foster kid."

"Well, you could tell them you had some family business to take care of, and if they ask further, just say that it was a personal matter. That is telling the truth without too much information, yes?" I was cool with that. I thanked her.

I spent the next few weeks getting caught up on school work and I played a lot with Traci and Scotty around the house. The Sweets were surprised at how much I could do, like cooking, cleaning and taking care of the kids. It was awesome having good food to eat all the time. At first, I felt guilty. I wished Angie, Tony and Matt could be here with me. But I had to stop worrying because I couldn't do anything about it.

Mrs. Sweet took me to buy some new clothes for school. She bought me some jeans, tennis and regular shoes, underwear, blouses, a couple of light sweaters, a sweatshirt, a pencil skirt and a red dress. I could mix and match all of them and make lots of different outfits. Mrs. Sweet was truly wonderful and she had good taste in clothes. I was in a daze over my new life.

Joanne was my only close friend in school. We never did anything outside of school, but we had several classes together and usually hung out at lunch time. I told her that I was living with the Sweets and they were my foster parents. It didn't bother her. She kept my secret close to her.

One day at lunch time, Joanne asked, "Mattie, have you met the new kid, Wayne? All the girls are going crazy over him."

"I've seen him several times, but never talked to him. He's definitely hot."

Later that afternoon, Wayne walked by me and said, "Hi, Mattie."

I was surprised that he called me by name. During the next few days Wayne would wave whenever he saw me. I wanted to talk to him, but he was always surrounded by other kids, mostly girls. Wayne was tall, with shoulder length blond hair and blue eyes. He was instantly popular, but he didn't seem stuck-up. He was definitely a hottie! I didn't understand why he constantly said hello to me. I wondered why he would be interested in me.

The next day I was walking to class and saw him waving at me. I started to wave back when someone pushed me from behind, right into a trash can! By the time I got out and turned to see who did it, they were gone. All I heard was some giggling. Wayne ran over to help me.

I was so embarrassed.

"Are you alright?"

"Yes, aside from smelling like rotten milk and cheese! Thank you for helping me. Did you see who pushed me?"

"Yes, but I don't know her name. I've seen her hang around with Rosie."

"Probably one of her gang members," I replied.

"May I walk you to your class?"

"I think I'd better go to the girl's restroom and clean up; maybe another time?"

"Sure. I'll see you tomorrow?"

"Great. See you then." My hands were sweaty.

Wayne caught up with me the next day as I was walking to class. He walked beside me and grabbed my hand. It surprised me. My stomach flipped and my hand tingled.

"You smell better today! I hope you don't mind me holding your hand. I've wanted to meet you ever since the first time I saw you."

I didn't know what to say, so I smiled and said, "Me too." Wayne started walking me to class regularly, even though he would have to run to his next class in order to get there on time.

One day at lunch, I asked Joanne, "Do you mind if Wayne joins us for lunch once in a while?"

Joanne looked at me with a grin and said, "Are you kidding? Of course I don't mind. You're so lucky! Everyone's talking about you guys."

On the way to my next class, a girl named Olivia bumped into me so hard I dropped my books and papers all over the walkway.

"Hey, watch where you're going," snapped Olivia as she kicked my books and papers farther down the hall. She leaned down beside me and said, "Stay away from Wayne, Bitch. He's Rosie's." I stared at her as she walked away.

Olivia was one of Rosie's gang members. Rosie was a "Bully" with a capital B. She had a gang of girls that did her nasty work for her. I heard that some girls in school had to *pay* Rosie in order for her to leave them alone. I didn't like where this was going.

That evening, Mrs. Sweet asked me if I would babysit the kids while she and Mr. Sweet went to a school board meeting after dinner.

"Sure. I'd love to," I replied.

"We'll only be gone for a couple of hours. Our cell phone number is on the counter in the kitchen," Mr. Sweet said.

I had already bathed the kids and was playing a 'Candy Cane' game with them when the Sweets returned home.

Scotty got up and ran to his mom, "Mommy, Mattie gave us a bath."

And Traci added, "She gave us ice cream, too!"

"Wow, that's wonderful. Thank you so much, Mattie."

Mrs. Sweet tried to pay me for watching the kids. I politely declined. I couldn't imagine taking money from them for babysitting after what they had done for me. They gave me an allowance every week and always paid for things I needed for school. They were more than generous.

Before I went to sleep at night, I always thought about my sister Angie and my brothers, Tony and Matt. I wanted to know if they were doing alright. I knew Louis was okay. He had called me a few times here at the Sweets. He was coming for Easter dinner. I couldn't wait to see him.

I'd called my mom a few weeks ago. She sounded distant and told me the kids were fine and so was she. She never asked me how I was. The old man must have been there because she sounded like she wanted to get off the phone. The call left me feeling sick to my stomach. I also had my recurring dream a couple of times after I spoke with her. My face would get hot and my temples would start pounding when I thought about my mom abandoning me for that creep. He had better not abuse Angie, Tony or Matt.

It was Friday at lunchtime when Wayne pulled me into the janitor's closet and planted a big kiss on me. At first it frightened me, but as we kissed, I tingled from head to toe. I had never had that feeling before. It seemed like time stood still. I felt so much love from Wayne.

"What if the janitor comes back and catches us?"

"He won't. He takes an hour break and leaves the school. I've checked it out. I've wanted to kiss you for a long time, Mattie. The first time I saw you, I wanted to be with you."

"I wish we could kiss for the rest of the afternoon," I said, as we kissed each other some more - until I remembered, "Oh crap! Joanne. She's waiting for us to have lunch with her."

We ran out of the janitor's closet giggling, holding hands and running to the lunch area. Joanne was waiting for us with a grin on her face. She was a pretty cool friend.

I was the happiest I had ever been. I loved the way Wayne looked at me, the way he walked and talked, the way he kissed, and I loved the way I felt when I was with him.

"Do I have to wait until Monday to see you again?" asked Wayne.

"Yes, but I hope this weekend goes by fast!"

"Can I call you, then? What's your cell number?" Wayne asked as he pulled out his cell phone.

"I don't have a cell phone, so... can I call you?"

I wasn't sure if I should give Wayne the Sweets' phone number without asking their permission. I didn't want to mess up a good thing.

"Okay, but you're a real mystery to me, Mattie," he said as he gave me his phone number.

"I'll explain my mysteriousness to you over the phone this weekend, okay?"

He walked me to my next class. We moved away from each other by sliding our hands apart. I couldn't believe the hottest guy in school liked me. I sure liked him.

Olivia walked by, shoved a note into my hand and ran off. I

opened the note. It read, "MEET ROSIE AT THE FLAG POLE TODAY AT 3PM AFTER SCHOOL." I thought about ditching my last class to avoid Rosie, but then realized I would have to confront her sooner or later. Sooner would be better.

Mr. Sweet always took about 20 to 30 minutes at the end of the day to gather up his stuff, so I only had a few minutes to get this over with. I walked to the front of the school and looked over at the flagpole. Not only was Rosie there with her arms crossed in front of her, but *so was her gang of four girls! Crap!*

I locked eyes with Rosie. As I approached her and the gang, I felt beads of sweat on my upper lip. I wiped them off with my hand. I'm glad I told Joanne about this. She would be watching as my witness and be ready to call a security guard or someone to help me. My heart was pounding and my legs were wobbly, but I wasn't going to show any fear. Besides, I decided there was *nothing* these girls could do to me that would even *match* what I had already been through.

As I got closer to Rosie, I noticed a small gang symbol tattooed between her right thumb and her forefinger. It looked homemade – ouch. I walked right up to her, put my belongings on the ground to the side of me, and said calmly, but firmly, "You have five minutes. What do you want to see me about?"

Rosie looked at me like she was confused. I'm sure she was used to kids being visibly scared or not showing up at all. She lowered her arms and pointed at me.

"You were told to stay away from Wayne. Don't let me see you with him again," Rosie said in a loud voice so the crowd gathering around us could hear her.

"Or?" I challenged.

I was definitely scared, but I concentrated on keeping my legs still. I remembered reading about warrior Indians. No matter how petrified they were, they never, ever showed fear, and they looked their enemy straight in the eye. I looked Rosie straight in the eye. I could tell it freaked her out a little. I thought about how I dealt with Marselda in Juvy. I knew I could deal with Rosie, but her gang, too?

"Or, you're going to have to deal with the consequences," Rosie said as she raised her right hand to hit me.

I grabbed her hand before it made it to my face and said, "Rosie, if you like Wayne, why don't you tell him? That's between you and Wayne. If he wants to be with you, I'll back off, okay? But if he *doesn't* want to be with you, will *you* back off?" I kept looking her in the eye.

Rosie's girls moved in closer. I didn't move. Rosie stared at me for a moment, cocking her head to one side. I sensed she didn't quite know how to proceed. Then she smiled and said, "You know, I like you, Mattie. I thought you were going to be a whiner. You're a tough girl. Who are you, anyway? Where are you from?"

"I'll tell you sometime, Rosie. It's probably not much different than where you are from.

Right now, I've got to go. See you on Monday?" I leaned down to pick up my things hoping she and her gang would let me leave without more drama.

As I walked away, Rosie yelled, "Yeah, see you on Monday, girl-friend. By the way, I don't want Wayne. He's yours."

I smiled back at her and booked it to Mr. Sweet's room. I made it just in time. He was ready to leave.

"TGIF, Mattie. Are you ready for a fun weekend?"

"Yes Sir, I'm ready!"

Louis came over for Easter dinner. He had Mr. Sweet for a math class a while back, so they already knew each other. Mrs. Sweet and the kids fell in love with Louis. The Sweets' let me call Mr. and Mrs. Outen. I wasn't supposed to, but they understood the situation. Louis and I both talked with them. Mom let Louis stay with Ken's family. I told Mrs. Outen how wonderful the Sweets were and all about Traci and Scotty. I also told her about Wayne and the situation with Rosie and her gang.

"Well my dear, you certainly deserve the wonderful things that are happening to you," Mrs. Outen said. "I would love to meet the Sweets someday, and Wayne, too! And, honey, Wayne sounds like a great guy, but don't go too far with him. You know what I mean?"

"Yes, I understand, and I won't."

"Honey, I heard that your brother Tony is in Juvenile Hall. He was picked up by the Police for stealing candy at Albertson's food store. Maybe you can ask Mrs. Astor to check on him for you. Other than that, it's been pretty quiet at your mother's house. I think the old man is working again. He leaves every morning and doesn't return until evening."

I was silent for a moment. A big lump formed in my throat.

"Are you there, honey?"

"Yes, I'm sorry. I try not to worry."

"My dear, don't worry about things you have no control over. It's wasted energy. Pray for them. That's about all you can do, but it will help."

I knew that was easier said than done.

The Sweets let me give their phone number to Wayne. I called him and told him almost the whole story. I didn't tell him that the old man tried to molest me.

"In a nutshell, I'm in a foster home. Mr. Sweet is my foster dad. He and his wife are really cool. I left an abusive situation and don't ever want to go back, although I miss my brothers and sister."

"Did you run away?"

"No, I went to Mrs. Henson and told her I didn't want to go home. She took it from there."

"Wow, I never would have known. You seem so together. It had to be awful for you."

"There are only three other people that know about my situation, Mrs. Henson, Mr. Sweet, Joanne and now you. Please keep it to yourself, okay? No one else needs to know."

"Of course, it's no problem. I think you're awesome, Mattie. I can't wait to see you."

Wayne and I became closer through the end of the school year. His family was going away for the summer to a relative's home in Montana. He wouldn't be back until just before school started in early September. We vowed to write and phone each other.

At the end of June, Mr. Sweet received a call from his mom. She had fourth-stage colon cancer and needed serious treatment. She would be coming to live with them.

That evening, the Sweets' told me about the phone call.

"This is something we never expected. We are so sorry we don't have room for you both, Mattie. We have enjoyed you being here with us. We are all going to miss you so much. We called Mrs. Astor this morning. She'll look for another home for you," said teary-eyed Mrs. Sweet.

Mrs. Astor had two weeks to find me another foster home or I would have to go back to Juvy. Mr. Sweet had talked to a few other teachers in school about becoming foster parents. Mr. English was a choir and music teacher. The next day, Mr. English said he and his wife would take the training and home study to become my next foster parents. I knew Mr. English, but had never met Mrs. English. I knew that she was a grade school English teacher.

Mrs. Astor made everything happen. She was amazing. Two weeks later, she picked me up on a Friday. It was a tearful goodbye at the Sweets. Traci and Scotty were crying and well…everyone was crying.

Mrs. Astor drove me to the English's home up in the Simi hills. On the way, she told me that Mrs. English seemed to be a rather serious person, and they had one son, Owen. She said he was quiet during her visit. My stomach was in knots. I hoped they would like me.

Chapter 5

End of August 2006 - Mrs. Astor drove me to foster home number two in Simi Valley. The long driveway led up to a plain, white ranch style home with a well-manicured lawn. It was the last week before school started. Mr. English answered the door.

"Hello, come on in," he said.

"Mr. English, you and Mattie already know each other. And who is this hiding behind you?" Mrs. Astor asked, as a young boy slithered around to the front of Mr. English.

"This is Owen. Owen, this is Mrs. Astor and Mattie. Mattie is going to be staying with us. Please, come in."

Mrs. Astor asked, "Hello, Owen. It's so nice to meet you. Is your mommy home?

Owen didn't respond, so Mr. English replied, "She won't be home for a couple of hours. She's preparing her classroom for next semester."

"Well, please say hello for me. Here's my card. I have to be going. Mattie, take care and I'll see you soon. Thank you, Mr. English."

"Well, Mattie, let me show you to your room, and then I'll show you around the house." Mr. English was short, slender, and bald on top with reddish-blond hair cut real short around the sides and back. He had blue eyes, thin lips, and freckles. He was nerdy looking.

Owen was eight years old. He stayed behind Mr. English while we walked around the house. Owen was thin and wiry with short, spikey blond hair and freckles on his face. He had amazing bright, aqua-blue eyes and thin lips. He looked like a quirky cartoon character out of the Sunday comics.

My new room was small. It had a single bed, a nightstand and a dresser all lined up around the walls. The closet was small, but I didn't have that many things, anyway. There was a small lamp on the nightstand and a clock radio on the dresser. Mr. English and Owen walked me around the rest of the house. The furniture in every room was lined up around the walls and open in the middle. It looked as though they hadn't decided how they were going to arrange it. The kitchen was extremely neat and tidy. Not much on the counters except for a toaster and a blender. There were no decorations - anywhere. The house felt dull, like there was no life in it. The walls were white and the furniture throughout the house was beige and tan with no color. The only color in the whole house turned out to be Mr. English and Owen's blue eyes. Too weird, I thought.

Owen moved right up into my personal space, looked up into my face, pinched me on my arm and ran away laughing hysterically.

"Sorry about that, Mattie. He's just excited. Is your room okay?"

"Yes, it's great. Thank you,"

"Mrs. English won't be home for another hour or so. I'll have to put some dinner together."

"What are you going to cook?" I asked.

"Well, there's some chicken and carrots in the refrigerator and, I don't know, maybe some potatoes."

I jumped in and said, "I can help you. I've been cooking since I was 10."

Mr. English showed me where everything was in the kitchen. I gathered the chicken breasts, the carrots, some potatoes and spices. I cooked the chicken with onions in a pan, made mashed potatoes, and steamed the carrots. Mr. English set the table while Owen buzzed around the kitchen like a bumble bee. I wanted to make a good impression on Mrs. English. Mrs. Outen told me you only have *one* chance for a *first* impression.

A while later, I heard a car door close, and brisk footsteps coming up to the front door. Mr. English and Owen seemed antsy. My heart started pumping pretty hard. In came Mrs. English. She put her purse and briefcase down on the hall table.

"Mommy, mommy, mommy!" yelled Owen, as he ran up to her and threw his arms around her hips.

"All right, all right, calm down," Mrs. English said, as she pushed Owen away from her.

She had on a white short-sleeve blouse, a navy pencil skirt and navy pumps with diamond stud earrings, a gold watch, and a simple gold wedding band. She was petite, with small beady eyes and thin lips. This was the "thin lips" family. Her auburn hair was short and brushed back on the sides. She was unpleasant to look at and be around.

"Alice, this is Mattie," said Mr. English.

Mrs. English slowly looked me up and down. I couldn't believe how rude she was.

"It's nice to meet you," I politely responded.

"You may call me Mrs. English. Something smells good. Let's eat."

We all sat down at the table. Owen sat next to his mom with his hands in his lap as though he were waiting for further instructions. Mrs. English pulled his plate over to her and appropriately filled it, making sure none of the foods touched each other. We ate in silence for a short time before she spoke.

"Albert, you've never cooked like this before. Did you use a recipe?"

"Mattie cooked this dinner for us. She told me she's been cooking since she was 10 years-old. Isn't it good?"

"Is that so?" Mrs. English said as she slowly put her fork down next to her plate and looked at me. I felt the mashed potatoes get stuck in my throat. Here we go with mashed potatoes again, I thought. She gave me a piercing look.

"Let's get something very clear, right here, right now, Miss Mattie. This is MY kitchen. From now on, you will not touch ANYTHING in MY kitchen without MY expressed permission. Am I perfectly clear?"

"Yes, Ma'am."

I barely got the words out. I put my hands in my lap. My face got hot. I felt like my heart fell out of my chest, rolled on the floor over to her, where she proceeded to stomp on it. My throat started closing up and I could hardly breathe. She continued.

"I want you to know something, Miss Mattie; I didn't want to take you in. Mr. Sweet had unfortunately coerced my "milquetoast" husband into it. But, since you are here, you will do *what* I tell you to do, *when* I tell you to do it, and *how* I tell you to do it. Understood?"

Mr. English said, "Alice, I don't think…"

Mrs. English moved her glaring stare from me to him. He stopped talking.

I almost expected her eyes to turn red, and her voice to get low and creepy, like an evil entity speaking through her. She stood up, picked up her plate, walked over to the trash can and dumped it. I stayed quiet. Owen was humming with his head down, moving back and forth in his seat. I felt tears welling up in my eyes. I tried hard to stop them. I didn't want to give her the satisfaction of seeing me cry. She grabbed Owen by his shoulder and told to him to go wash his hands. He leaped up from his chair and whirled down the hall toward the bathroom. I felt deeply sorry for Owen. She was so nasty and cold. I felt so uncomfortable. I didn't know what to do. I was freaking out.

"May I help you clear the table?" I asked in a very humble way, trying to soften the mood.

She didn't respond. She ignored me and proceeded to pick up the dishes, one-by-one, dumping all of the remaining food in the trash. I was shocked. All that good food was *gone*. The leftover chicken could've been made into creamed chicken or into sandwiches for the next day.

Mr. English sat there like a statue and said nothing. Oh no, I thought. I'm in a reverse situation from the house I had escaped from.

"May I be excused?" I asked.

She very curtly said, "You may."

I went to my room, sat on the bed, and stared at the wall. My first three hours in this house had been a nightmare. I couldn't believe Mr. English would bring me into a house like this! She's a monster.

I shouldn't be here, I told myself for the umpteenth time. I should take it all back, go home, and pretend none of this ever happened.

The rest of the weekend I spent a lot of time in my room and taking care of Owen. The poor kid was starved for attention. The only attention his mother gave him was negative, like ordering him to do something, or telling him to sit down and be quiet. Owen had a perpetual look of someone smelling rotten pickles.

Mrs. English wanted me to play some games with Owen one evening. We started playing Checkers. He lost the first game and went into a screaming rage. He picked up the checker board and flung the board and the checkers into the air. Then he ran into my room, pulled out a box of my pictures from the closet, and started to tear them up. I grabbed him and tried to calm him down. Mrs. English came in yelling.

"What are you doing? You're supposed to *let* him win. He's just a kid, for God's sake!"

From then on, I changed the way I communicated with Owen. He wouldn't stay still long enough for me to read to him, so I started drawing with him. At first, he only wanted me to draw him animals. I did, but I would leave something out, like one leg or eyes. He would grab the pad from me and fill in the missing parts. Then he would look at me and grin. That became our new thing to do. Every night he wanted to sit with me and draw. On the weekends, when I wasn't cleaning, I would take him outside and play ball with him. We would chase each other around the yard. He loved it and so did I. I loved to hear him giggle.

One afternoon, I noticed Mr. English watching us from the living room window. Later that evening, Mr. English told me he was happy to see Owen having such a good time. He thanked me. Mrs. English never said anything unless she was giving orders. I think she was just using me as a servant and babysitter. I either cleaned the house or took care of Owen.

One Saturday morning, Mrs. English told Mr. English to cut the grass. Owen and I were at the kitchen table eating peanut butter and jelly sandwiches. Well, we had the peanut butter on one plate, the jelly on another and the bread on still another plate. Owen never wanted his foods to touch each other. It drove him nuts. So, I did the same thing to make him happy.

We heard Mrs. English out on the lawn yelling at Mr. English. The lawnmower had crapped out and he didn't know how to fix it.

"You idiot - can't you do anything right? You'd better borrow a lawnmower from a neighbor and finish the job. I will NOT stand for a half-mowed lawn!"

As Mrs. English stormed through the front door, Owen put his arms around my hips and squeezed. I took him to my room to draw. I noticed that Owen's left eye would twitch when his mother yelled at his dad. To get his mind off of his mother, I turned the radio on and sang along with some of the songs. After that day, Owen wanted me to sing along with songs on the radio whenever we were drawing. His eye would stop twitching.

One evening, Mrs. English told me I was going to watch Owen while they went to a school meeting. Everything was fine until I tried to put Owen to bed. He had a raging, screaming fit, running through the house. I grabbed the drawing pad and asked him very calmly, "Do you want to draw, Owen?"

He said, "NO. NO. NO!"

"What do you want to do, Owen? It's time to go to bed. It's sleepy time."

"I want to sleep with you," he replied with his usual rotten pickle face.

"I tell you what; I'll lay down with you on your bed until you go to sleep, okay?"

He was fine with that. The only problem was; I fell asleep on his bed. Mrs. English woke me up by poking me in my side. She followed me to my room.

"You will not, ever again, sleep on Owen's bed. Is that CLEAR?"

"He was scared. I told him I would stay there until he fell..."

"That's enough, Miss Mattie. Don't' you talk back; it's obvious that you're trying to turn Owen against me. It will stop immediately; do you understand me?"

"Yes, Ma'am," I said, half asleep. I thought about calling Mrs. Astor the next day. I'd rather be in Juvy than here in this madhouse with this monster woman.

Wayne and I could only see each other in school. I wasn't allowed to give the English's phone number to anyone and I could not have anyone over. I didn't want to, anyway. Both Wayne and Joanne agreed I had already been at the English's too long. It had only been a few weeks, but I needed to get out of there. I also noticed that they *never* had any company over to their house and the phone never rang except for anything having to do with school business.

I had to ask Mr. English for money to buy lunch at school. I didn't dare make my lunch in *her* house. She never offered or mentioned the subject. She basically treated me like wallpaper. Actually, she treated everyone in *her* house like we were intruders. She was the monster, Mr. English was her puppet, and Owen was the loon. It was sad.

I missed my sister Angie and my brothers. I hoped she was okay. I tried to remember their faces when I thought about them because they were starting to fade in my mind. Mrs. Astor told me that both of my younger brothers, Tony and Matt were in foster care. I felt my stomach clench. Had my mom *totally* lost it? I was so angry with her and the old man, I couldn't stand it. I tried real hard not to think about it. It wasn't easy.

One day in Drama class, a girl named Julie Anne Savoy came up to me and said,

"Hi Mattie, do you have a minute? I'd like to talk to you."

The boys in school called Julie Anne 'Tits-ma-grits' because she had big boobs. She was tall and slender with long dark, wavy hair and slightly crooked teeth. I didn't know much about her other than we helped each other rehearse once in a while. She played piano in the school orchestra. She seemed okay.

"Sure, what's up?"

She sat next to me, leaned over and whispered, "I know about your situation with the English's. I overheard a phone conversation Mr. English had with his wife about you. I feel for you. Mrs. English is a total bitch. How...

I interrupted her. "Wait a minute. Why would Mr. English have a conversation about me in front of any students? Were you snooping?"

"I was the only one near him when he was on the phone. No one else heard anything. It must be hell living in that house. How would you like to come and live with *my* family? My parents have been foster parents before. My older brother, Billy, is in the Marine's. So, it's just me, my mom and dad. Would you like to, at least, meet my parents?"

I sat there staring at Julie Anne and thinking about how miserable it is at the monster's house. "Sure, but I'll have to get permission from Mrs. English."

"Just let me know. I've already told my parents about you and they would like to meet you," she said.

This was all so sudden. I didn't really know Julie Anne. I just knew her from our Drama class. I heard her playing piano one day when I was walking by the music room. I stopped to tell her how well she played. I think it made her happy that someone gave her a compliment.

That evening at dinner, Mrs. English said, "Mrs. Astor will be coming here this evening, Miss Mattie. I told her she needs to find you another place to live. It's not working out for you, here."

I didn't say anything. I finished eating and thanked her for my meal. She was a horrible cook. Her food tasted as bland as her house looked.

"Don't try to butter me up, Miss Mattie. It won't work."

Maybe this was what you call "good timing." She beat me to it, dang. I could tell that Mrs. Astor was surprised at what Mrs. English had to say about me when she came by that evening. Mrs. English bad-mouthed me in the worst way. She told Mrs. Astor that I was a bad influence on Owen and that I was trying to turn Owen and her husband against her. I knew Mrs. Astor didn't believe any of it. Mr. English had called Mrs. Astor before she came over and told her that his wife was the problem, not me. He also told her that Owen loved being with me and that I had spent a lot of quality time with him. He had become a happy kid while I was there and he was worried about what would happen to Owen when I was gone. Mrs. Astor recommended that *he* take over with Owen where I left off. Wow, Mrs. Astor was a smart woman.

"Mrs. Astor, I'm very sorry this didn't work out," Mrs. English said with the usual cold tone in her voice. "How soon do you think it will take to find her another place to live?"

"I'm working on it, Mrs. English. I'll be in touch."

I walked Mrs. Astor out to her car. I told her that Mrs. English was lying. I had developed a wonderful relationship with Owen. He had some serious problems and they wouldn't deal with them. I explained everything that had happened while living with the English's and how close I had become with Owen. I told her that Owen had become much calmer and focused since I had been there, and I would miss him.

"Don't worry, Mattie. I know what's going on. I believe you. Mr. English confirmed everything you just told me. Don't give it another thought."

I was relieved. I told her about Julie Anne Savoy talking to me in Drama class. She was surprised and very interested, of course. She said she would check it out for me. I gave her the Savoys' address and phone number.

It was the first Sunday in November when Mrs. Astor took me to meet the Savoy family. Mr. Savoy was an executive with a big rocket engine-building corporation. He was a big man with a big ego. Mrs. Savoy was a breast cancer survivor and seemed very nice. Their big house was up in the hills of Simi Valley. I would be sharing a bedroom with Julie Anne and she seemed to be happy about it.

Their house was huge with a big, beautiful entry way, a blue and cream living room with a grand piano in the corner, a big dining room and kitchen, a fair sized family room, three bedrooms, a den, and three bathrooms. I wouldn't understand why Julie Anne wanted to share her room with me until later. I didn't ask. I was happy to have another place to live.

Mrs. Astor had filled the Savoy's in on my story. Mr. and Mrs. Savoy both said they would be happy for me to come and live with them. When I returned to the monster's house, I couldn't pack fast enough.

Mrs. Astor picked me up at 5:00PM on Friday to take me to my third foster home.

After the last of my belongings were put into Mrs. Astor's vehicle, I walked back to the front door to say goodbye to Mr. and Mrs. English and Owen. Owen had his face stuck in Mr. English's side. He wouldn't look at me.

"Mr. English, thank you for giving me a place to live for a while. Owen, I will miss you so much. Mrs. English, your heart is *dark*. Owen needs *love* not *abuse*. Please get your family some help."

As I was saying this to the monster, she sucked air and her eyes bulged out. I was proud of myself for confronting her. I had thought about what I was going to say to her for two days. I rehearsed it over and over like it was a part in a play. It was my best performance, ever.

On the way to the Savoy's house, I told Mrs. Astor that I was sorry she had to continue finding places for me to live and I hoped this one will be the last until I turned eighteen.

"Mattie, think about it, I haven't found any homes for you. Your teachers and your school mate, Julie Anne, have done it for us. And it's all because of the good person you are. Just remember that. It has been a pleasure for me to help you."

"Thank you for everything, Mrs. Astor. I am so fortunate to have you looking out for me."

"You are welcome, Mattie."

I wish I could've been there that night when Mrs. English sat down at the dinner table. Owen and I had put a "fart cushion" under the pad on Mrs. English's chair.

Chapter 6

November 2006 – I was a freshman in Simi Valley High School. Julie Anne and I were getting to know each other. We rode the bus together to and from school. Julie Anne played the piano for about an hour every evening while I sat and talked with Mrs. Savoy. Mrs. Savoy seemed happy to have someone to talk to. Mr. Savoy worked long hours. When he returned home each night, he wanted to eat dinner and retire to his den for the rest of the evening. Mrs. Savoy didn't cook very often. She preferred to buy meals at the grocery store or from a restaurant. I offered to cook, but she told me she was happy with the way she handled the meals. I didn't think she believed that I could really cook. I let it go.

Mr. Savoy took all of us out to dinner at a nice restaurant for Thanksgiving.

The food was awesome. We brought home enough leftovers for the next day. I enjoyed the meal, but I was feeling overwhelmingly alone. I missed my sister and brothers so much.

Mr. Savoy monopolized the conversation by talking about how important his job was and how difficult it was to manage hundreds of employees. Mrs. Savoy, Julie Anne and I listened like we were *really* interested. Cough, cough.

It was close to Christmas and Julie Anne was now used to me being around. She stopped spending time with me. She drove to school with an older girlfriend that had just received her first driver's license. I continued to ride the bus. Joanne was still my school pal. Wayne's family moved back to Montana to be near their relatives. I missed him. We wrote for a while and then it faded. I wouldn't be surprised if he had a new girlfriend.

Mrs. Savoy was good about letting me call Mrs. Outen once in a while. I could talk for fifteen minutes. We caught up on news with each other. She said it looked like my mom was hanging in there. I wondered if and when I would see my mom again.

One night Julie Anne told me she was going to go out our bedroom window to meet her friends. Friends - meaning a football player or two? I didn't know for sure.

"I'm going to put pillows under my blanket to make it look like I'm here. Don't say anything to my parents. They never come in to see if I'm here, so it shouldn't be a problem."

"What am I supposed to tell them if they *do* come in?"

"Don't worry. They won't. Just pretend you're asleep," she said as she slowly opened the bedroom window and climbed out.

I couldn't sleep that night, but I was ready to pretend if her parents came in our room. I worried about Julie Anne. What was she doing out there? I thought it was unfair of her to do this to me.

Julie Anne was good about not letting people know that I lived with her family as a foster kid. At least, that's what I thought, until one night when she told me the *real* reason she wanted me to come and live with her family. I was deeply disappointed.

"I wanted you to come and live with us so my parents would focus their attention on you instead of me. That's what they did with the last foster kid we had, and it worked. My dad won't let me go to parties or social events unless they have to do with Job's Daughters. My dad is a Mason."

"What is 'Job's Daughters?" I asked. "And, what is a Mason?"

"The Freemasons are a secretive fraternal society that was started back in the early 16th Century in Europe. It is supposedly built on Brotherly Love, Belief, and Truth. Masons must declare belief in a supreme being and they must maintain good moral and ethical values. Job's Daughters are sponsored by the Masons for girls aged 10 to 20. It's supposed to build character through moral and spiritual development"

I asked, "Is it a certain religion?"

"No. We welcome many religions and cultures."

"Could I join Job's Daughters?"

"You could if you were related to a Mason and he sponsored you. You could search both subjects on the internet and learn all about it. Anyway, my dad is very strict about what I do and what you do."

"I wish you would've told me this before I came here, Julie Anne. I don't think it's fair that you brought me here under false pretenses, do you?"

"Are you kidding? You were in a nightmare house and I rescued you. Wouldn't you rather be here than back with the English's? Besides, you won't have to lie for me. Just tell them you were asleep and didn't know what I was doing."

"Of course, but please don't ever ask me to lie to your parents for you."

"I will never ask you to lie to my parents and you won't have to because you don't know what I am doing, right? It's a non-problem. I will have your back, no matter what, okay?"

All I could do was trust her and that was sort of hard to do. I didn't see any spirituality in Julie Anne or her parents. I guessed she did the "Job's Daughter's" thing just to keep her dad off her butt. So now, I had to keep quiet about her sneaking out at night and whatever else she did. I felt stuck in this situation. I didn't know what to do. Maybe I'd call Mrs. Astor. This sure was a strange family.

The next day at lunch, Joanne told me, "Kids are saying that Julie Anne is meeting some of the football players late at night and having sex with them. I don't know if it's true, but that's what they're saying. They're calling her "promiscuous Julie Anne." The guys talk about her big boobs."

"Yeah, she sneaks out at night sometimes, but she won't tell me anything, and really, I don't want to know."

That night, I asked Julie Anne if she had one boyfriend or if she was seeing more than one guy. I shouldn't have asked her, but I was curious.

"It's better if you don't know anything about what I do, Mattie. I won't ask you about what you do; deal?"

"Deal, but I don't like it."

It was the evening of January 6, 2007 and I was sitting on my bed feeling bad that no one told me Happy Birthday. I figured if the Savoy's cared about me at all, they would know today was my birthday and I turned 15. Mrs. Outen and my brother Louis sent me cards.

Mrs. Savoy handed me the cards and said, "Here's a card from Mrs. Outen and one from your brother. That was nice of them. What do they say?"

I opened the card from Louis and said, "It says, Happy Birthday. Yesterday, I turned fifteen."

"What! Oh my, Mattie. Happy Birthday! I am so sorry, I didn't know. Well, I'll tell Mr. Savoy and maybe we'll take you out for a birthday dinner. Does that sound like a good idea?"

"That's okay. I appreciate you telling me Happy Birthday."

That night, Julie Anne turned over in her bed and said, "Hey, I'm sorry we didn't know yesterday was your birthday, Happy Birthday. Don't worry, things will get better."

"Thanks," I went to sleep missing my sister Angie and my brothers. I wondered if they were missing me.

That Saturday night, the Savoy's took me out for my birthday to the same great restaurant where we had Thanksgiving dinner. Mrs.

Savoy handed me a card with a twenty-dollar bill in it with all three signatures.

"Thank you all so much. I really appreciate it," I said.

Louis called me two days after my birthday to say hi and tell me he was sorry he forgot to call on my birthday. I didn't care. I was so glad to hear from him. I told him things were going okay for me. He got a part-time job at the Simi Valley Bowling Alley. He was still staying at Ken's house. He said he hadn't spoken to Mom and didn't really care to.

I woke up on Sunday morning and saw that Julie Anne was not in her bed, but it looked like she *had* been there. Concerned, I got up and got dressed. It seemed awfully quiet in the house. I went to the bathroom. Every time I went to the bathroom since Juvy, I was happy I could close the door and have some privacy.

I walked all through the house. Everyone was gone. I looked for a note and found nothing. I walked into the garage and saw that the car was gone. Why would they go somewhere without me? I hoped there wasn't an emergency and they forgot to wake me up. I hung out in the house all day and into the early evening. I was really worried. Something must have happened! I couldn't go anywhere without their permission, so I was stuck in the house until they returned. I didn't have any of their cell phone numbers, so I couldn't call them. I kept the phone beside me all day waiting for them to call.

Later that evening, I heard Mr. Savoy's voice and the keys in the front door lock. All three of them came in.

I met them at the door, "I was worried about you guys. I thought maybe something had happened."

"Everything's fine. You were sound asleep this morning. We didn't want to disturb you," Mrs. Savoy said.

That *really* sounded strange to me. It upset me that they didn't even leave me a note. It just isn't right, I thought. I thought that maybe they were testing me to see if I would stay in the house until they returned or if I would take off without their permission.

A few months went by and I studied hard in school. I took extra credit classes. I was only a freshman, but I knew if I worked hard and kept getting high grades, I'd be able to graduate early right after I turned eighteen and be on my own. I would also be ready for college, if I wanted to go.

One night, when Julie Anne and I went to bed, she rolled over and said, "I saw Mr. English today. I asked him how it was going. He asked how you were doing and said that Owen really missed you. He told me that you and Owen put a "fart cushion" on Mrs. English's kitchen chair. When she sat down at dinner that evening, the fart cushion went off. Owen started laughing hysterically, pounding his hands on the table."

"Really?" I laughed. "Did he say what Mrs. English did?"

"He said, at first she stood up, pulled the cushion out from under the chair pad, sat back down, and then started laughing hysterically as well. He asked me to tell you thanks for doing that. It was the first time they had all laughed together."

I lay in bed trying to visualize the scene. It made me happy that it ended with all of them laughing. That was so cool! It certainly wasn't the way I thought it would end. Maybe things would slowly get better for them, especially Owen.

Mrs. Astor stopped by to check up on me and the Savoy's. I had a chance to talk to her alone at her car when she was ready to leave.

"Mr. and Mrs. Savoy seem very nice. They had nice things to say about you, Mattie. Are you happy here?" she asked.

"It's okay. What did Mr. Savoy say about me?" I asked.

"He said you were being respectable and making good grades."

I wasn't expecting anything better than that from him. I told Mrs. Astor about why Julie Anne wanted me to live with her family and about her sneaking out the bedroom window at night. She didn't think that was so bad until I told her about the Savoy's leaving me alone in the house every once in a while on Sundays. She didn't say anything for a minute.

"Well, all you can do is stay home until they come back. You should ask them if they would leave you a note or allow you to call them on one of their cell phones."

I also told her what happened at the English's regarding the fart cushion. She laughed.

"Mattie, you're bad. That's very good news. Take care and call me if anything gets more out of line. I'll be in touch."

The next few months were fairly uneventful. School would be out for the summer in a few weeks. I wanted to get a part-time job like babysitting, but Mr. Savoy said we were all going on a two-week vacation to Washington State. I was looking forward to it. He said we would be camping outdoors and going water skiing on a lake. The only part of summer vacation I wasn't looking forward to was being alone almost every Sunday while the Savoy's went out. They would never tell me where they had gone. Strange, I thought. It made me feel like I was definitely not worthy to be a part of their family and it hurt. I was going to ask them to leave me a note, like Mrs. Astor recommended. I did and it didn't work. It was just too weird.

School finally let out for the summer. I got all A's and one B on my report card. I was happy. I showed it to Mr. and Mrs. Savoy. Mr. Savoy said, "That's the kind of report card we expect from you, Mattie. It's a good reflection on our family. Julie Anne got all A's. Bring that B up to an A next year."

"Yes, sir," I said. What a jerk, I thought. Mrs. Savoy didn't comment.

Thankfully, I hadn't had my recurring dream for quite a while. I missed Mom and my siblings. Mom never tried to get ahold of me. She didn't even send me a birthday card. I wished I could see Angie and give her a big hug, and I was worried about Tony and Matt being in foster care. I hoped they were being treated well.

I was getting excited about going camping in two weeks with the Savoy's. Julie Anne acted uninterested. I wasn't surprised. What I wasn't expecting, though, was what happened that Sunday.

Chapter 7

*J*une 2007 – There I was again – all by myself. The Savoy's left early in the morning, just like they did at least two Sundays a month. They didn't come back until later in the evening. I wasn't allowed to leave the house without their permission, so I read, did some homework, watched TV, and I got a little scared, too. I started chewing my nails. They were not a pretty sight. As always, I started to get bored. Little did I know that on this Sunday evening, I would be anything but bored.

It was about 9:00PM and very quiet – except for the TV. I kept it at a low volume so I could hear the Savoy's at the front door before they came in. Mr. Savoy always put his key in the lock and turned it quickly. I could hear them talking to each other as they came in. Mr. Savoy would look around, and then walk back to his den without saying a word.

Mr. Savoy was a cold person. He was certainly not the kind of person you would want to have a conversation with. He always knew more than you. He had no friends that I knew of.

Mrs. Savoy would always say, "How was your day, dear?"

"Fine, thank you," I'd reply, even though it wasn't true, and I was upset about being left alone.

Julie Anne would say, "Hey," as I shut the TV off, and we went to our bedroom. Then, she wanted to know what I did all day - really?

But tonight, I heard an unfamiliar noise at the front door. No one rang the doorbell. And no one was talking. I got up from the sofa and moved quickly toward the front door. The doorknob turned slowly to one side and then slowly to the other side, as if someone were checking to see if the door was unlocked. My heart started pounding fast. I swallowed hard and stepped back slowly into the family room. I turned and moved quickly into the kitchen to get the phone. The phone was on the counter that separated the kitchen from the dining room. I accidently knocked over a cup on the counter. I grabbed it to stop the clanking noise.

The shadow of what looked like a man, moved outside past the sheer curtains in the dining room. I curled up underneath the counter between a barstool and the wall, with the phone in my hand. I prayed the man couldn't see me. I could hear him trying to open the sliding glass door. The sliding door was right next to me, and it was locked. I always locked the windows and doors when I was alone.

As soon as he moved away from the sliding glass door, I crawled on my hands and knees through the kitchen, the family room, and down the long hall into the den.

I crawled behind Mr. Savoy's big recliner chair in the corner of the room and listened for the prowler. He came to the window in the den that was right beside the recliner that I was hiding behind. I could see his shadow moving across the curtain. I held the phone between my legs so he couldn't hear it. I dialed 911. My heart was pounding so hard, it hurt.

"What is your emergency?" the lady dispatcher asked.

"Someone's trying to break into the house," I whispered. My voice quivered.

"Did you see someone?" she asked.

"Yes, please help me! There's a man trying to get in," I felt panicky. My heart was pounding faster, and my hands shook. The lady asked me to confirm my address and give her my name. I confirmed the address.

"My name is Mattie. I'm here by myself."

"Your parents aren't home, Mattie?"

"No. They should be home soon. Please help me! He's trying to get in the window!"

"How old are you, Mattie?"

"I'm 15. Please hurry!" I pleaded.

"Mattie, help is on the way. Two policemen are very close to your street. Stay on the phone with me. Where are you in the house?"

I whispered, "I'm in the den in the back of the house behind a recliner chair in the corner."

"Mattie, I will help you through this. Where is the man? Can you see him?"

"I see his shadow at the window. The window is right next to the recliner chair. I'm afraid he will hear me."

"Mattie, Officer Harwood is now in front of your house. The other officer will check around the outside. Are you okay?"

"Oh no, he's trying to open the window," I gasped. My throat was so dry that I could hardly get the words out. I trembled. The prowler was taking the screen off the window. He slowly slid the window open and his hand reached through. I was scared, but anger suddenly flooded me. How dare this creep scare me like this? I shot up from behind the chair and slammed the window shut on his arm as hard as I could. The prowler yelled, "Son of a Bitch!" He pushed the window open again to pull his arm out.

I heard an officer say, "Down! Get down on the ground."

The lady on the phone said, "Mattie, go to the front door as fast as you can. Officer Harwood is there. Ask him his name. When he gives you his name, open the door. Do it quickly."

I ran through the house as fast as I could, falling a couple of times before I reached the front door.

"Who is it?" I asked.

"Officer Harwood, Mattie. Open the door."

I was shaking so much; it took me a minute to get the door un-locked and open. Officer Harwood took me outside while two more officers searched inside the house. There were three police cars at the house and four policemen. An officer came around the outside corner of the house with the handcuffed prowler! I sucked air when I saw him. The prowler had his head down. I'm glad he didn't look at me. I was so relieved. Officer Harwood put his arm around me and told me I was brave and that I did the right thing. It made me feel better - until I heard the Savoy's car coming up the driveway.

"What's going on here, Officer?" demanded Mr. Savoy.

"A prowler has been caught, thanks to your daughter. She called 911 as he was trying to break into your house," Officer Harwood said.

"She's not my daughter. She's our foster child. You said you caught the guy?"

"Yes, we have him in custody."

"Good. I'm not happy seeing all these police cars in front of my house."

I was being questioned by another officer a few feet away and didn't hear what Mr. Savoy was saying. Then I heard Officer Harwood raise his voice.

"Mr. Savoy, this young lady could've been seriously hurt this eve-ning. She was smart and brave enough to call for help. She is the reason we caught this guy. The prowler was coming in through your den window. She slammed the window on the prowler's arm giving us more time to apprehend him. I should think you'd be happy she's not seriously hurt. She's scared to death though, and could use a little comfort," said Officer Harwood sternly.

After the police were gone, Mr. Savoy called me into his den.

"Sit down, Mattie."

I sat down on an ottoman with my hands cupped over my knees.

Mr. Savoy closed the window and grumbled about having to replace the broken screen.

"I don't ever want to come home to police cars surrounding my house again. I don't know if you were doing something to lure this guy here or what. From now on, keep the windows, doors and drapes closed when we're not here. Is that understood?"

"Yes, sir, but I always lock the windows and doors when you're gone," I said, my voice quivering. I was still shaking. What he said pissed me off.

I wiped what I thought were my sweaty hands across my pants.

Mr. Savoy looked at me like he would crush me if I said another word. Then he looked down at my hands and said, "That looks like blood on your hands and pants."

"It must've happened when I crawled from the kitchen back to the den."

Mrs. Savoy came into the den, saw the blood and gasped.

"Take her to the bathroom and clean up the scrapes on her knees," Mr. Savoy told Mrs. Savoy. "You'll be okay, Mattie. The guy's behind bars by now," he said as though he were trying to be consoling. Mrs. Savoy took me to the bathroom and proceeded to clean up my scraped knees. They burned like they were on fire. I told her that I crawled on the floor from the kitchen to the den and I fell a couple of times running to the front door to let the officer in. I told her I was sorry about the blood on the carpet.

Julie Anne thought it was *so* exciting. She stood by the door listening with her eyes wide. I was glad she didn't want to sneak out of the house that night.

I wondered if what happened with the prowler would make the Savoy's feel guilty about leaving me alone on Sundays. Maybe they'd take me with them next time. What was the big secret, anyway? I had asked Julie Anne and Mrs. Savoy and they both give me a "brush-off" answer like "We just went for an outing." It drove me crazy, so I tried not to think about it.

That night, it took me a while to go to sleep. I didn't care for Mr. Savoy, however I felt safe with him in the house. He was a big, intimidating man that would scare anyone off with just his looks and attitude.

Julie Anne wanted me to give her more details about what happened that day.

"Please, can we talk about something else? I'm still shaking from today. I need to think about something else, okay?"

"Sure, have you ever been water skiing?"

"No, I haven't. Is it hard?"

"No, I think you'll do okay. It's fun. Are you looking forward to our camping trip?"

"Yes, I am. I've never been camping or water skiing before."

I worried about having to testify against the prowler in court. I hoped that wouldn't happen. I never saw his face. The officer told me some other neighbors around us had seen him and scared him off their properties.

I fell asleep watching the bedroom window.

Chapter 8

August 2007 – Mr. Savoy was silent as he drove us north to go camping at Lake Bryan in southeastern Washington. It was a long ride, so I brought along a book of short stories to read. Julie Anne stared out the window. She wouldn't carry on a conversation with me around her dad because she knew he wouldn't want to hear most of what she wanted to talk about – namely, boys. One night before we left the house, as she started going out the bedroom window, I whispered, "I hope you're protecting yourself if you're having sex."

She turned and looked at me as if I was from another planet and said, "Remember to mind your own business, and I won't tell anyone you're a foster kid in our house."

"I'm sorry, but I worry about you sometimes," I whispered as she climbed out the window.

We all left on vacation the next morning. The car was cold with the air-conditioning on high for Mrs. Savoy. She had hot flashes. She carried a fold-up fan in her purse and had one in each room of the house. The ride in Mr. Savoy's big Lincoln was like being in a cushy rocking chair. I pulled a sweatshirt out of my tote bag and put it on. On the way, we stopped at nice restaurants to eat. Mr. Savoy liked to be waited on.

On the long ride, I thought about my sister Angie and my brothers, Louis, Matt and Tony. I talked with Louis as often as I could.

He came by the Savoy's several times to see me. Mr. and Mrs. Savoy were very nice to him. I'm sure they liked Louis because Mr. Savoy told him he could come back anytime.

I hoped Matt and Tony were doing okay in their foster homes. I worried about them so much. I missed my mom. She taught me a lot, like making homemade bread and spaghetti sauce. My arms would get tired of kneading the dough for ten loaves of bread. All I wanted was to be outside playing with my sister and brothers. That was before the old man came into the picture.

Mrs. Savoy let me speak with Mrs. Outen before we left on this trip. I told Mrs. Outen about my guilt feelings after I eat and that I still worry about my brothers and sister. She responded by saying, "Mattie dear, don't worry about things that you have no control over. Concentrate on doing the right things for yourself. When something good happens to you, embrace it, enjoy it, because, Honey, you deserve it."

I wanted to tell Mrs. Outen that I had been feeling down a lot lately. She always made me feel better, but I didn't want her to worry about me. Sometimes reality sucks.

We arrived at Lake Bryan in southeastern Washington State around early evening. The sun was still bright. The camping area was not what I expected. I thought we would be camping in tall pine trees in sort of a forest setting. This place was along the remote Snake River with wide open vistas, steep canyon walls and few trees. It was desolate and dry, but the lake was nice and inviting. I couldn't wait to go swimming in it.

It was fun setting up camp. Mr. Savoy knew a lot about camping. We put up two tents, one for Julie Anne's parents and one for us. We put our sleeping bags and belongings in our tent. Then Julie Anne took me on a walk to show me the area. She said they camped there every year.

Mr. Savoy made a big fire that evening. A family of five that were camping near us came over and introduced themselves. The couple, Mr. and Mrs. Rivers, had three kids; a good looking eighteen year-old named Matt, a shy ten year-old girl named Trudy, and a cute eight year-old girl named Ruthie. Mr. Savoy invited them to roast marshmallows with us, and they accepted. Matt played his guitar, and we all sang cowboy songs. It was so cool sitting out in the open air by a big fire and singing songs as loud as we wanted to. Everyone was happy.

Julie Anne unzipped her sweatshirt in the front to partially expose her "girls." She sat at an angle so that her dad couldn't see her breasts, but Matt could! Mrs. Savoy thought it was so sweet that Matt was paying special attention to her daughter. Matt was tall and slender, with dark brown curly hair and big brown eyes. I finally had a chance to watch Julie Anne in action. She giggled at everything Matt said and smiled bigger than ever.

Mr. Rivers invited all of us to go water skiing the next day. Mr. Savoy accepted his offer and even smiled when he shook Mr. River's hand before we all retired for the night. Mr. Savoy acted like a nice human being on this trip. He even talked to me once in a while, mostly to tell me what to do and how to do it, but he was nice about it. Mrs. Savoy and Mrs. Rivers hung out together. I spent time with Trudy and Ruthie playing games like "Hide and Go Seek." Julie Anne and I took walks and went swimming. For the first time in a long time, I felt that life was good. I was soaking it all in.

The Rivers' had an 18-foot Haskell Hull boat with a 360 cubic inch AMC engine, pushing a panther jet. It was fast. I watched everyone else water ski before I tried it. Mr. Savoy gave me some tips. "Keep your knees together, hold on tight to the handle and let the boat pull you up," he said. It worked. I stayed up all around the lake on my first try. It was more fun than a person deserved!

Julie Anne snuck out of our tent at night to meet Matt after everyone had retired.

I could tell she really liked him. She was smiling a lot. She was happy, and that was good.

"What do you think of Matt?" she asked me one night.

"I think he's a nice guy, and he seems to like you a lot. I'm happy for you."

"I'm sorry that I've been such a bitch. You've had my back, and I do appreciate it. Matt was concerned that he was taking too much of my time away from you. I told him you were a close friend that was spending the summer with me, and that you were okay with it. I hope you are okay with what I told him."

"I guess, if it's true, I mean, that we're close friends," I said with a grin.

"I've never really had a close friend, so I guess you're the closest I've come to having one," she said, as though she surprised herself by saying it. Then she continued.

"I don't know if my parents said anything to you, but I graduated early. I'll be starting college the first week in September. I'll be moving to the college dorm."

"What college?" I asked.

"University of California, Santa Barbara, UCSB," she responded.

And then it hit me, "That's just three weeks away! I wonder why your parents haven't said anything."

"They'll probably tell you on the way home. They wanted you to enjoy this vacation."

"I don't understand. Am I going to be staying at your house or going to another foster home?"

"I'm not sure. They haven't said anything to me about that," she said as she yawned. "Let's get some sleep. We're going skiing again tomorrow with the Rivers."

I wondered why she would tell me that, now. It took me a long time to go to sleep. I had the old recurring nightmare, again. I woke up during the night all sweaty and scared. I looked over at Julie

Anne. She was sleeping like a baby. I wondered how someone like Julie Anne, who had more than she could ever want, had no clue how to treat people.

I wondered if the Savoys had already spoken to Mrs. Astor.

Fortunately, the last few days we spent camping were busy with water skiing, swimming, campfires, and games. The Rivers appreciated me spending time with their two young girls.

We all spent the last night around a big campfire eating grilled hamburgers and fried potatoes that Mr. Rivers cooked. It was the best hamburger I had ever eaten. There were a lot of "mmm's" going on.

The next morning after a bacon and egg breakfast cooked on the fire, we took down the tents. Everyone was quiet. We packed the car and then went to say goodbye to the Rivers. Everyone vowed to stay in touch with each other. I saw Matt slip something into Julie Anne's hand as we departed. It made her smile. I thought maybe she would show it to me later.

The ride home seemed much longer than the trip going to the campgrounds. We stopped to eat dinner at a fast-food place. We were almost done eating when Mr. Savoy looked at me and said matter-of-factly, "Mattie, Julie Anne is going away to college in a few weeks. We called Mrs. Astor before we left on this trip to see if she could find you another place to live. Mrs. Savoy and I will be doing some traveling. I told Mrs. Astor you may stay with us until she secures a place for you. You're a nice young lady, Mattie. I hope you stay that way. We hope you've enjoyed staying with us."

Mrs. Savoy said, "We've really enjoyed having you stay with us, haven't we, Julie Anne?"

"Yeah, it's been nice," Julie Anne replied.

The last French fry I ate stuck right in the middle of my throat. I got up and ran to the rest room to get rid of it. Julie Anne followed me.

"Are you okay?" she asked.

"Yeah, I guess I'm a little shocked. Sorry."

Julie Anne handed me a paper towel and said, "Well, I'm sure Mrs. Astor will find a good place for you."

"Sure," I said. "Like the English's? By the way, did Mr. English tell you I was his foster kid? Is that how you found out?"

Julie Anne crossed her arms in front, lowered her head, then looked at me for a few seconds and said, "Listen, I'm going to tell you something that you have to promise me won't go any further than this bathroom, okay?"

"Do I have a choice?" I said sarcastically.

"Mr. English has had a crush on me for a long time. Each day after choir class, he would talk to me about his unhappy home life and the situation with you. I think he just needed attention. I sort of used it to my advantage. He gave me an 'A' even though I would skip class a lot."

"What do you mean, the "situation" with me?"

"He thought that having you at the house would neutralize the drama with his wife and Owen. It didn't work. Mrs. English was super jealous of you. She thought you were trying to turn Owen and Mr. English against her. What can I say? She's a psycho. Hey, don't worry; I'm sure you'll get a decent place."

"Wow. Did he ever make a move on you?"

"No, he's too much of a chicken. He just liked being near me, I guess. But, he sure told me what a cold bitch his wife was. He said their bedroom was the coldest room in town. That was more information than I wanted. Poor man, he is so unhappy."

We arrived home late that evening. Mr. Savoy said we could unload the car the next day. It was a relief. We were all very tired from having so much fun.

I lay in bed hoping I would move to another place in the same town so I could stay in the same school until I graduated. I had been taking a lot of college prep courses so I could graduate early like Julie Anne did.

I started getting angry at my mom, again. This was all her fault. I thought about my brothers and sister as I fell off to sleep. She chose the old man over us kids. That's sick.

The next morning, as I was getting dressed, I noticed something sticking out of Julie Anne's purse on the dresser. It was about a 3-inch piece of wood with a heart carved on it. It had Julie Anne and Matt's initials in the heart. That was what he had slipped in her hand. How cool was that. It made me think about Wayne. I wondered how he was. I missed him.

Mrs. Savoy answered the telephone, and then handed it to me.

"Hi Mattie, this is Mrs. Astor. How are you?"

"I'm fine, Mrs. Astor. How are you?" I asked.

"I'm good, thanks. I have someone I want you to meet, Mattie. Her name is Mrs. McNeedy. She has a new two-story home here in town. She has no children, but is interested in meeting you. Can I pick you up tomorrow morning at 10:00AM?"

"Sure, I'll be ready," I said.

"Great. I look forward to seeing you, Mattie."

Oh no, I thought. Here I go again. Mrs. McNeedy, a woman with no children? What if we don't hit it off? What if she doesn't like me? Why would she take in a teenage foster kid?

Chapter 9

September 2007 – On the way to Mrs. McNeedy's house, Mrs. Astor asked me how I was doing.

"I'm okay, I guess," I said.

"Are you sad because you're leaving the Savoy's?"

"Yes and no," I said.

"Explain what you mean, Mattie."

I told Mrs. Astor about how cold Mr. Savoy was about the prowler incident and that the family pretty much treated me like wallpaper. And, they wouldn't tell me where they went on the Sundays they left me alone. And now they were done with me. I felt like a piece of meat, and it hurt.

Mrs. Astor replied, "You know Mattie, you may *never* find out where they went on Sundays when they left you alone, but think about it; even if they told you, you might be disappointed in what they had to say and wish they *hadn't*. Have you and Julie Anne become good friends?"

"Not really. Julie Anne only wanted me there so her dad would focus on me and not her. That way, she could pretty much do what she wanted without him noticing, and it worked.

The only close friend I have is a girl in school named Joanne. She knows about my situation and is quiet about it. I've missed her this summer. The Savoy's wouldn't let me have anyone over except my brother, Louis. Mr. Savoy liked him. Louis came over a few times to visit."

"I'm so glad you're seeing Louis, Mattie. The Savoy's are a little different, but try not to take everything that happens personally. I think that's just the way they are. Mattie, you're getting taller and prettier every time I see you. I bet you are getting looks and winks from lots of boys!"

"Thank you," I responded. I knew my breasts had filled out and I had a nicely shaped body, and I hadn't bitten my nails for a long time, until this ride to Mrs. McNeedys. I was definitely nervous.

We pulled into Mrs. McNeedy's driveway. It was a plain two-story tract home with a nice lawn. There were no flowers, just a few green bushes up against the house. We heard a dog barking inside. The door opened and a lady wearing black-rimmed, coke-bottle-bottom glasses greeted us, "Hi, come on in! Stop it, Little Girl, stop it. Sorry, this is Little Girl. She's really a sweet dog. She'll get used to you. Come in and sit down."

We followed Mrs. McNeedy into her living room. Mrs. McNeedy's eyes looked huge through her glasses, almost like big cartoon eyes. She had black hair that was brushed straight back in waves that ended mid-neck in the back. She wore a white blouse with small pink polka-dots on it, an A-line blue denim skirt, white slip-on tennis shoes, and no makeup or jewelry. She asked me to come and sit next to her on the sofa. When I did, she leaned forward to look at me up close. It sort of freaked me out. I almost laughed, but stopped myself.

"My, you're a very pretty girl," she said.

"Thank you," I replied, as I felt my face flush.

"Mrs. Astor has told me all about you. You are an "A" student and have never been in trouble. That's commendable, dear. My husband, Frank, is a traveling salesman and is only home one weekend a month. He'll be home next weekend. It gets rather lonely around here sometimes. So, you're going to be in the 10th grade?"

"Yes, Ma'am, I start next week, I mean, if I get to stay in the same school."

"Oh, you can call me Mrs. M," she said, patting my hand that rested on my thigh.

I figured Mrs. M liked me because she took me and Mrs. Astor on a tour of her house. We went upstairs first and straight ahead to a small bedroom that had a single bed, a dresser, and a small desk with a lamp on it. There was a hall bathroom and another bedroom that she said was her husband's office. We followed her back downstairs to the kitchen. It was nice and big with forest green appliances and oak wood cabinets. Then we walked down a short hall past a bathroom to her den that had a big fish tank filled with tropical fish.

We walked down a hallway past a green colored door that had a deadbolt on it. She didn't say anything about that door so we proceeded to go back into the living room. There were mini-blinds on the windows, but no curtains. It was a fairly new home. The living room was filled with big, neutral-colored, furniture.

Mrs. Astor excused herself as she had to get going to another appointment. She thanked Mrs. McNeedy and said she would call her in the next day or so. I leaned down to pet the miniature poodle, Little Girl. She responded by licking my hand.

Mrs. Astor pulled out of the driveway and asked me, "Well, what do you think?"

"I'm not sure. Truthfully, she freaked me out a little. Is she the only possibility I have?"

"Yes, I'm afraid so, Mattie, but you'll be able to stay in town and the same school. I think she just needs someone to take care of and keep her company while her husband is out of town."

"Have you ever met Mr. McNeedy?" I asked.

"Yes, he's a nice person. They are both nice. They have been fos-ter parents twice before to younger girls. Both girls ended up going back to their families."

I wanted to talk to Mrs. Astor about how I had been feeling, but she had to rush off to her next appointment. I was getting frustrated. Mrs. Astor was far too busy.

"I'll be in touch after I talk with the McNeedy's. I think it will be a good change for you, Mattie. Hang in there."

She dropped me back at the Savoy's. I went straight to my bedroom and sat on the bed. Julie Anne was sitting in a chair in the corner of the room reading.

"Well, how did it go? What is Mrs. McNeedy like? Tell me everything," she said as Mrs. Savoy came in.

Mrs. Savoy asked, "How was it, Mattie? I didn't have a chance to speak with Mrs. Astor. She just dropped you off and left."

"She was late for another appointment. She said she'll call in a couple of days."

Again, Julie Anne said, "Well, tell us all about it. What's she like, what's her house like?"

I suddenly felt a pain in my chest and overwhelming emotion. My face got hot. Then I blurted out, "You guys are just *curious*. YOU DON'T REALLY CARE! It was WEIRD, okay? She was weird."

I started crying uncontrollably. Julie Anne came over to the edge of her bed and sat across from me. I started yelling, "Why is this happening to me? I'm sick and tired of moving from place to place. Why does my mom let this happen to me? I'm not a bad person. I'm NOT a bad person!"

"Of course you're not a bad person, Mattie," said Mrs. Savoy. "I'm sure Mrs. Astor will make sure you go to a good home. Why, in about two years, you'll be on your own! And I think you'll do very well."

"Mom, let me talk to Mattie alone, please," Julie Anne said as she dismissed her mom with a wave. As her mom left the room, Mr. Savoy came through the doorway.

"What is going on, here?" he said in his usual controlling man-ner. Julie Anne looked up at her dad and shook her head at him. Mrs. Savoy mumbled something to him and they walked out, closing the door behind them.

To my surprise, Julie Anne sat there while I balled my eyes out. She didn't say a word. She handed me some tissue. I cried for a long time with my face in the pillow. I slowly sat up holding my head. It hurt.

She stood up and said, "I'm going to get you something for your head, okay? I'll be right back."

She was back in a flash. "Here, take this," she said, as she handed me some pills and a glass of water. She sat down on her bed again, looked at me and said, "I'm here if you want to talk."

I took the pills and drank the water. "I'm so tired of being treated like a stupid juvenile. I've never really felt a part of any of the families I've lived with. I'm always the "odd one-out" and it sucks. I'm sorry Julie Anne, thanks for staying and talking with me."

"You know, I never really thought about what you have been through and how it would feel to be bounced around strange fami-lies. One thing I do know for sure is that you're not a stupid juvenile, and I'm sorry you have to go through this. You've been more of a friend to me than anyone ever has. I wish I could wave a magic wand and make it all better for you, but I think you're going to do just fine. I'm glad you came to stay with us and I will actually miss you, but don't tell anyone I said that!"

I half smiled and said, "I'm sorry I blew up. I can't believe I did that. I've been feeling so down lately. I think Mrs. McNeedy looks weird, but I'm sure she's alright. At least I won't have to deal with other kids. It'll just be me, if she takes me in, that is."

Julie Anne surprised me by saying, "She will. Hey, promise you'll write me occasionally and let me know how you're doing. I'll give you my address at the college dorm before you leave. Will you?"

"Sure, I will if you'll write back."

"Deal," she said.

"What are you going to major in?"

"Music, of course; "I'll be trying out for the college orchestra. I'll miss my piano."

"And I'll miss hearing you play. Every time you practiced, I would sit around the corner in the family room and listen."

"Really?" Julie Anne said with a surprised look on her face.

Two days later, the phone rang. It was Mrs. Astor. She spoke with Mrs. Savoy for a minute before Mrs. Savoy handed me the phone.

"Hi Mattie, Mrs. McNeedy really liked you and wants you to come live with her and her husband. So, what do you say?"

"When do I start packing?"

"How about I pick you up on Friday at 1:00PM?"

"I'll be ready, and thank you, Mrs. Astor."

Thursday evening was my last night at the Savoy's. They took me out to dinner.

"I want to thank you for taking me out to dinner. It means a lot to me. Thank you all for everything." Then I asked, "Would you tell me where you went on the Sundays you left me at home?" All three of them just stared at me in silence.

"Okay, never mind," I said with a grin.

Mr. Savoy told me to keep up the good work in school. Mrs. Savoy asked me to write her and let her know how I was doing.

That night, as I put a sweater that my mom had given me into my suitcase, something fell out. It was a handkerchief. I held it up to my face and savored my mom's pleasing scent. She must've put it inside the sweater before I left the house. Even though I never wore it, I kept lugging it around because she gave it to me. It brought a flood of emotions back into my head and my heart. I missed her so much, it hurt. I missed my family. I hated the old man.

The next day, Mrs. Astor pulled into the driveway. Julie Anne gave me her address at the college dorm and helped me load my things into Mrs. Astor's car. She gave me a hug. No words, just a hug. Mr. and Mrs. Savoy told me to take care of myself and waved from their front door.

As I watched them wave at me, I thought, *"There goes another piece of my life."*

I'm headed to foster home number four. I wondered what it was going to be like to be the only kid in a big house. I wanted to talk to Mrs. Astor about my feelings of depression. I wanted to tell her that I blew up at the Savoys, but she was in a hurry, as usual. I felt numb. I hoped Mrs. McNeedy wouldn't be as weird as she looked.

Chapter 10

September 2007 – My stomach churned and grumbled as we pulled into Mrs. McNeedy's driveway. I hadn't eaten all day. I was too nervous. Mrs. McNeedy came out to greet us. Mrs. Astor and Mrs. McNeedy helped me unload my belongings from Mrs. Astor's car and take them up to my new room.

"Well, looks like you're all set, Mattie," Mrs. Astor said, once we were back downstairs. "I'll check in with you in a couple of weeks. You have my phone number. Mrs. McNeedy, I'm sure you'll enjoy having Mattie stay with you. Have a good weekend."

"Thank you, Mrs. Astor," I said, as we watched her pull out of the driveway.

"Thank you for taking me in, Mrs. McNeedy."

"You can call me Mrs. M, Mattie. And, you're quite welcome. Let's get you unpacked."

After unpacking my things, only one-third of the closet and two of the dresser drawers were filled. There was a little girl's outfit hanging in the closet. I pushed it to the other side and wondered if it had belonged to one of the other foster kids the McNeedy's had.

"My dear, you don't have many clothes, do you?"

"I don't need much. It's easier when I have to move."

Mrs. M pulled that little girls outfit out of the closet and said, "I hope you like this outfit. Isn't it cute? Try it on when you get a chance. I bet it will look good on you."

I was stunned. I looked at her to see if she was joking. She wasn't. That outfit would fit a little girl of about ten or younger. I told myself she might be overly excited about me being there. I responded by saying, "Yes, it's cute."

Later, Mrs. McNeedy called me down to the kitchen to sit and talk to her while she fixed us something to eat for dinner. She prepared a dish called "Hungarian Goulash." It was beef in a gravy sauce over buttered noodles. It was awesome.

While we were eating, Mrs. M proceeded to tell me, "I do all the cooking and cleaning in my home, and I take care of Little Girl and the fish tank. Little girl is not allowed on any furniture, so don't let her up on your bed. I want you to keep your room and bathroom clean and concentrate on your school work. I will do the laundry. I have a gardener that takes care of the outside. He comes every Tuesday. Do you have any questions?

"When will I meet Mr. McNeedy?"

"He'll be home next Friday evening for the weekend. I'm sure he will like you, Mattie."

"Are you done eating?"

"Yes Ma'am, it was delicious. Thank you."

"I'm going to take you shopping tomorrow for some new school clothes. Would you like that?" she asked.

Surprised, I said, "Yes, thank you."

Mrs. M cleaned up the kitchen while I sat there answering questions about my other foster families. I made her think every foster home I had been in was wonderful. I asked if I could help her clean up. She told me that she would take care of the cooking and cleaning.

We watched television that evening before I went to bed. I lay there in a strange bed, in a strange house, thinking about the weird thing that happened with the little girl's outfit. It made me think of my sister Angie. I missed her, my brothers and my mother. I cried myself to sleep thinking about how my mother abandoned me.

I was totally unprepared for what happened the next day on our shopping trip.

Mrs. M had my breakfast ready. She served it to me, cleared my dishes from the table and washed them. She wouldn't let me help her. That felt strange to me.

She took me to a local mall. I followed her into a department store's clothing section for children. I thought maybe she wanted to buy something for a relative's kid or something. I was confused. She led me back to a sales rack and started pulling out one outfit after another, saying, "Oh, isn't this cute" and "This one is so adorable. Do you like them?"

"Yes, they're nice. Are you looking at them for a niece or?" I said.

"No, dear Mattie, for you, I don't have any nieces. What do you think of this dress?" Her excitement was starting to creep me out. At first, I thought it was a joke, but as I watched her, I realized that she was very serious.

"Well, Mrs. M, this dress isn't my size. I'm 15 years old. I wear a size 9/10. This is way too small for me." Without trying to upset her, I held the dress up to my body so she could see how small it was. The situation was getting a little nutty.

"Don't you at least want to try it on, Priscilla?" she said with her magnified eyes glaring at me through her "coke-bottom-bottle" glasses.

"My name is *Mattie*, Mrs. M. Are you okay? My size clothing would be in the Misses section." I guessed Priscilla must have been her last foster child.

Mrs. M stared straight ahead for a moment, put the dress back on the rack and said, "Oh, you're right. What was I thinking? Let's go to the Misses section."

I was relieved. Only temporarily, though. We went to look at my size clothing. She picked out the most foo-foo, frilly clothes, and had me try every one of them on. I went along with it for a while until I just *had* to say something.

"Mrs. M, these clothes are nice, but very uncomfortable for me. Do you mind if I show you something that *would* be comfortable for me?" I asked as delicately as I knew how. I didn't want to sound ungrateful; however, I didn't want the clothes she picked out.

She allowed me to show her some pieces that I liked. Reluctantly, she agreed to buy them for me. I started paying closer attention to her after that clothes buying session.

She took me to lunch at a nice restaurant in the mall. I noticed that the waiter wouldn't look at Mrs. M. I think her eyes behind those glasses were hard for some people to deal with. She had told me she was almost blind without them. She couldn't wear contacts, so she was stuck wearing the glasses. I felt bad for her. She was very quiet while we ate our lunch.

"Mrs. M, are you upset with me?"

"No dear, I was thinking we need to get home. I need to feed Little Girl and take her outside."

On the way home, we talked about me starting school on Monday and the courses I would be taking. The next day, she bought me some school supplies. I spent the afternoon in my room reading. I went downstairs to ask Mrs. M if I could have something to drink. I had to ask her if I wanted anything, even a glass of water. I couldn't find her so I yelled for her. I was standing in the hall outside of the den. I heard her voice behind the green door. She came out holding the door close behind her like she didn't want me to see what was inside the room. She quickly locked it and put the key in her dress pocket. I must have looked confused.

Mrs. M nervously said, "Oh, this is my private room where I uh...store my things."

I wondered why she was acting so strange and what was so secretive about that room, and why was there a deadbolt?

My first week back in school was going well. I saw Mr. Sweet and told him that I was in another foster home and it was nice. He was happy to hear that. He said his mom's cancer had gone into remission, but she was going to continue to live with him and his family.

Mrs. Henson, the school Counselor, called me into her office and surprised me with a hug. She wanted to hear about the Savoy's and the McNeedy's, and wanted to know if I was okay. I assured her that I was doing great.

I was so happy to see Joanne. We hugged and squealed. We had several classes together. I told her about moving from the Savoy's to Mrs. McNeedy's. I planned on asking Mrs. M if I could have some company over once in a while.

My first two weeks with Mrs. M were, at best, unusual. She waited on me, did my laundry and made my school lunches. The first lunch I opened had a happy face carved into the apple. I showed it to Joanne. She looked at me with a scrunched up face and said, "Isn't that sort of weird?"

"Yeah, I think so. Mrs. M is a little strange. She treats me like a little girl. I am not allowed to do anything but keep my room and bathroom clean. She does everything else. She doesn't even know that I can cook, clean and sew. She treats her poodle named Little Girl just like a kid as well. Joanne lifted her eyebrows.

I told Joanne all about the little girls outfit, the shopping trip, and about the room with the green door that I was forbidden to go in to.

"Are you going to try to sneak into that room to see what's in there?"

"I don't know. I *am* curious about it."

"Mattie, the little girl's outfit, the shopping trip, the carved happy face on your apple – that's a little wacko. You said she had other foster kids before you?"

"Yes, I think they were a lot younger than me. But, I'm not really sure."

On Friday evening, the front door opened, and in came Mr. McNeedy. He was HUGE.

He was over 6 feet tall and weighed about 350 pounds or more. He waddled over to the sofa and sat down, breathing hard. Mrs. M pushed me in front of him and said, "Honey, this is Mattie."

"Hi, Mr. McNeedy, it's nice to meet you."

"Hello, Mattie. I'm Frank," Mr. McNeedy said as he wiped his sweaty forehead with a handkerchief. "Sweetie, will you get me something to drink?"

"Sure Honey," Mrs. M said as she motioned for me to follow her into the kitchen. While she poured a drink for Mr. M, she said, "Mattie, on the weekends that Frank is home, I want you to stay in your room. It's the only time I get to spend with him. I'll bring your meals up to you. Except for Sunday, we'll all eat dinner together. You understand, don't you, dear? He'll be leaving on Monday morning before you get up."

She handed me a bottle of water and motioned for me to go up to my room. I was flabbergasted! As I started up the stairs to my room, I heard Mrs. M tell her husband that I liked staying in my room and reading. Not!

That weekend, I read, I wrote poems, listened to the radio, took little naps, cleaned my room, my bathroom, ate the meals Mrs. M brought up to me and did exercises, trying to make the time go by faster. I couldn't wait to talk to Mrs. Outen and tell her about this looney house.

I felt like I was being held hostage in a tiny hotel room. Mrs. M brought me a tray of food and told me to put the tray outside the door when I was finished for her to pick up. I couldn't help but feel like an intruder in the house.

On Sunday morning, she came to pick up the breakfast tray and said, "Mattie dear, Frank and I are going for a ride. We'll be back in about an hour or two. If you want, you can watch television until we return."

I watched them leave in Mr. McNeedy's big Cadillac. They took Little Girl with them. I waited until they were out of sight and went straight to the green door. It was locked. I went to the McNeedy's bedroom to look in the pocket of the dress Mrs. M was wearing the day before; no key. Then I got a flashlight out of a kitchen drawer. I kneeled down on the floor with the flashlight trying to look under the door. It didn't work. I put the flashlight back exactly where it was and watched more television.

I called Mrs. Outen. She laughed out loud as I told her all about this crazy house and the McNeedy's. I hoped it wouldn't get worse.

"Honey, be careful about the green room. If you get caught, it may ruin your chances of staying with the McNeedy's. But, now you have *me* curious about that room. You must call me and let me know when you find out what's in there. Oh dear, I shouldn't be telling you that!"

I hung up the phone when I heard the car doors shut. I ran upstairs to my room, grabbed a book, turned on the radio and sat at my desk.

Mrs. M came up to my room to say they were home and for me to come down for dinner at six. So strange, I thought. I felt like I was in a boarding house. I went down for dinner precisely at 6:00PM. Mrs. M had made steak, baked potatoes and corn for dinner. It was so good. She was a great cook.

Mr. McNeedy was fun to talk to. He told us some interesting stories about his travels and I answered lots of questions about my family and the foster homes I had been in.

I couldn't wait to get to school the next day. School was my sanctuary. It was the only place where I felt normal and safe.

I looked forward to being free of my bedroom for the next three weeks until Mr. McNeedy came home again. Mrs. M was creepy nice and this house was the most mysterious place I had ever been in.

I wanted to know what was behind the green door.

Chapter 11

October 2007 – Mr. McNeedy was gone before I got up on Monday morning. Mrs. M called me down to the kitchen for breakfast.

"Frank left before you got up, Mattie. He said to tell you that he is glad you're staying with us."

"Thank you, Mrs. M. I enjoyed listening to him talk about his sales trips during dinner last night. He sure loves your cooking and so do I," I said, enthusiastically.

She smiled and looked at me with those big cartoon eyes as she handed me my lunch. I left for the school bus stop. On the way to the bus, I wondered what weird little thing she had put in my lunch that day. It ended up being a peanut butter and jelly sandwich cut out in the shape of a bear. She must have used a big cookie cutter.

During lunch with Joanne, I cupped my hands around the sandwich as I ate it, so no one could see the bear shape.

That Saturday, my brother Louis and his friend, Ken came over to see me and meet Mrs. M. My brother impressed her with a small bouquet of autumn flowers. She served us hot cider and oatmeal chocolate chip cookies. Then she proudly displayed the flowers in a vase on the coffee table. We talked for over an hour. When Mrs. M excused herself to take Little Girl outside to do her business, Louis said that Mrs. Outen had told him what I had told her about Mrs.

M and this crazy house.

"Are you going to be okay here, Sis?"

"I think so. She's wonderfully creepy, but she's good to me," I whispered.

Ken said, "I'm glad you're in a nice home. Louis worries about you all the time."

"Thanks, Ken. I'm okay. I'm so glad you and your dad are letting Louis live with you."

"We gotta go, Sis. I'll see you soon," Louis said as they both looked down the hall at the green door and smiled at me.

Mrs. M came back in, thanked Louis for the flowers, and invited them back anytime.

Louis replied, "And, thanks for the delicious cookies and cider, Mrs. McNeedy."

She smiled and said, "I'm so glad you enjoyed them."

I felt a sad tweak in my heart as I walked Louis and Ken out to the car. I tried not to cry when Louis gave me a hug and said, "Hang in there, Sis. I love you."

"I love you, too, and miss you already."

I stayed in my room for the rest of the afternoon feeling alone and depressed. I missed Louis, Tony, Matt and Angie.

Mrs. M called me down for dinner. She made another delicious dinner of fried chicken, mashed potatoes and roasted winter vegetables. We watched television that night. I asked her if I could sleep in the next day. She agreed and said that she would fix something quick for breakfast like cereal and toast. I thanked her and went to bed.

A few minutes later, I heard her go into the green room and close the door. I wondered what was going on in that room. I became more curious and decided that since I lived here now, and I needed to know.

The next day, I didn't get up until 10:00AM. Mrs. M had a bowl of cold cereal and some fruit waiting for me. She sat and talked with me while I ate. Even though Mrs. M. treated me like a little kid, she made me feel special and wanted.

"We'll go grocery shopping when you're done eating, Mattie. Do you need anything else for school?" she asked.

"No, but I appreciate everything you've done for me, Mrs. M."

After grocery shopping that afternoon, I helped carry the bags into the kitchen and she unpacked everything. I went to my room to read. About an hour later, I heard a loud crashing sound coming from downstairs. I ran down to see if Mrs. M was okay. I heard her moaning behind the green door. The odor coming from that room was a horrible stinky, chemical smell. I rushed through the door and saw Mrs. M on the floor. I leaned down to help her, but she started screaming at me, "GET OUT OF HERE! GET OUT OF HERE, NOW! GO!"

I quickly left the room, but on the way out I glanced at a couple of pictures of young girls hanging above the table. On the table were some bins with chemicals in them. It was sort of dark in there with a red light hanging over the table and one over a bench. I guessed it was a "dark room" where she developed pictures. I didn't understand what the big secret was, although, I thought I saw the girls in those pictures wearing the little girl's outfit that hung in my closet. It gave me the creeps. I was pretty shaken. What was that all about, I wondered? After that incident, I was done worrying about the "green room."

I went back up to my room and stayed there until she called me down for dinner. We ate quietly until I said, "I'm sorry, Mrs. M, but I was worried that you had been hurt. I heard a big crash and I heard you moaning."

"It's alright, dear. I was angry that I fell and spilled some chemicals. But, in the future, you don't go in that room unless I ask you to, no matter what, understand?" she said in a cool tone. "That is my *private* space."

"Yes Ma'am," I replied.

We never spoke of the incident again.

Mr. McNeedy came home for the four-day Thanksgiving weekend. I guess they felt bad that I was stuck in my room the whole time, so they surprised me with a small television with specific instructions regarding when I could and couldn't watch it. I was happy to receive it. The holidays were the hardest time for me. I ached for my family and I grew to hate the old man more and more. And my mother; I hated her, too. I made a life decision that Thanksgiving weekend. I would *never* have children and I would *never* end up like my mother. When I turned eighteen, I would be in control of my own destiny. I would be successful and help other kids.

In December, I was in a Christmas play at school. Mrs. M had taken me to and from each rehearsal and did the same for every performance. She even brought her camera on opening night and took pictures of me in the play. I looked over at her. She wore a big smile. It made me happy to have her there. Then, I noticed two girls from Rosie's gang standing in the aisle making fun of Mrs. M and her thick glasses. I walked over to them and whispered, "That lady happens to be a friend of mine. Don't be disrespectful." I looked both of the girls straight in the eye.

"Sure, sure, Mattie, we don't mean no disrespect, sorry," one girl said as they both scurried away.

Ever since the incident at the flag pole with Rosie the bully and her gang, they had treated me with respect. Rosie tried several times to befriend me, but I politely declined. She was still doing some bad things like making shy kids pay her every day to "keep them safe." The school administration was aware of it and didn't do anything about it. I asked Rosie to stop doing it. Her response was, "Mattie, if any of those stupid kids would just tell me to leave them alone, and *mean it*, I would. But, they don't. So they pay me and I make sure they don't get hurt. Have a nice day, girlfriend."

Mr. M. came home for a few days over Christmas. Mrs. M told him all about the Christmas play and showed him the pictures she took. He told me he was sorry he didn't get to see the play, but he enjoyed looking at the pictures.

After dinner one evening, I heard Mrs. M calling for Little Girl. I went downstairs.

"I can't find Little Girl," Mrs. M yelled in a panic. She noticed the front door was ajar. "Oh, dear me, she must've gone out the front door!"

Mrs. M told me to stay in the house while she and Mr. M. went out to look for the dog. They came back twenty minutes later and said they would have to get in the car and go looking for her. They told me to stay in the house in case the phone rang. Little Girl had a collar with her name and the McNeedy's phone number on it.

I watched their car pull out of the driveway and head down the street. I walked back down the hallway toward the den to be by the phone. As I passed the green door, I tried the doorknob. It was open! I pulled the door open just enough to look inside and then slowly went in. My eyes slowly adjusted to the dim lighting. There were several photos of little girls hanging on the wall. They all had the same outfit on. It was the outfit Mrs. M hung back in my closet! The one she tried to get me to try on. She had also called me Priscilla a few times. I found several photos with the name "Priscilla McNeedy" written on the back. It was her child! Her daughter must have died. I picked up a box from under the bench. It had used little girl's panties, socks, and small stuffed toys in it. I looked on the back of the pictures hanging above the chemical bins. Every one of the pictures had "Little Girl" written on the back, but no names. And, all of the girls were wearing that same outfit! Two of the girls looked unhappy. The outfit was way too small for them. It looked like they were crammed into it. It was weird and creepy.

I heard a car door shut. I moved quickly out of the room and into the den. I sat next to the phone and pretended I had been there all along watching television. It had been on the whole time. They came in with Little Girl. They found her a few blocks away. Everyone was happy.

The holidays were hard for me. Christmas was just around the corner. I felt the pain of being alienated from my family even more during the holidays and it made me angry. As wonderful as the McNeedy's were to me, I was still depressed.

However, I was surprised on Christmas Day! Mrs. Outen, Louis and Ken came over to visit. Mrs. M had secretly invited them over to cheer me up. Mrs. M had hors d'ourves and spiced cider for all of us. Mrs. Outen had left her two boys with Mr. Outen. She brought over some of her homemade Clam Dip. It was so good, Mrs. M asked her for the recipe. We all sat around and told stories, laughed, and enjoyed the goodies. I didn't want this day to end. I didn't want them to leave, ever.

Mrs. Outen asked me to show her to the restroom. As we walked down the hall, she saw the green door and whispered to me, "Honey, you'll have to fill me in when we walk to the car!" We giggled.

That was the best Christmas I had had in a long time. Even though Mr. McNeedy was home, I didn't have to stay in my room. Mrs. M liked Mrs. Outen and ignored the fact that I wasn't supposed to talk to her or see her until I was eighteen and on my own. It was great having Christmas with my brother and my friends and I loved Mrs. M. for making it happen for me.

Before I went to sleep that night, I thought about what I saw behind the green door. The pictures of those girls crammed into that little girl's outfit and the horrid looks on their faces. I hope she doesn't try to make me put that outfit on.

The more I thought about it, the creepier it felt. Poor Mrs. M., she had lost her *only* child and hasn't gotten over it. That must be why she called me Priscilla several times. I felt so sorry for her, but the situation seemed to be getting worse, and Mr. M. didn't know what was going on.

Chapter 12

January 2008 – I turned sixteen the first week in January. I received cards from Mrs. Outen, Louis, and Joanne. Mrs. M made me my favorite cake - chocolate with chocolate frosting. It was amazing. I opened two gifts from her. One was a pair of small teddy bear pierced earrings. I guessed she didn't notice that I didn't have pierced ears. The other gift was a teddy bear necklace that was for a little girl. I couldn't get it around my neck.

"Let me put it on for you," Mrs. M said. "Why, you have a big neck, Mattie. I'll have to find a longer chain. Do you like the earrings?"

"They're really cute, Mrs. M. Thank you."

"Try them on so I can see them on you."

"Mrs. M, I'm sorry, but I don't have pierced ears."

"You don't have pierced ears? Oh my, I didn't know that. I'm sorry, Mattie. I tell you what, we'll go and have your ears pierced this weekend. Would you like that?"

"I don't want to hurt your feelings, Mrs. M, but I don't want my ears pierced."

"Alright then, we'll take this jewelry back to the store and exchange it for something else." She served us some cake and chocolate ice cream. We watched television until it was time for me to go to bed.

"Thank you so much for the cake and presents, Mrs. M. I really appreciate it."

"You're so welcome, Mattie."

I went upstairs and she went into the green room. I heard her lock the deadbolt from the inside. After what happened the last time, I asked her *not* to lock it, because if anything happened to her while she was in there, I couldn't get in to help her. But, I decided I wasn't going to go down there and get yelled at.

Something woke me up in the middle of the night. I opened my eyes and almost screamed. Mrs. M was standing beside my bed staring down at me. I rubbed my eyes and pulled my brain together as best I could.

"Mrs. M! Is everything okay?"

"Yes, Priscilla, I was just watching you sleep. You looked so peaceful. I didn't mean to wake you. Go back to sleep, now," she whispered. Then she tucked me in and left the room. I sat up in bed, shocked at what had just happened. It took me a while to get back to sleep. I had the recurring nightmare about the old man. I woke up again, sweating and shaking.

I was tired the next day in school. Joanne was really concerned when I told her what happened the night before.

"She is flipping out, Mattie!" Joanne blurted out. "That is freaking scary. What are you going to do?"

"I don't know. Mr. McNeedy will be home this weekend. I'm hoping he will help her work it out after I tell him what is going on. And, I hope she doesn't get mad at me."

"Promise me, if anything wacko happens, you'll call the police."

"I think she needs help, that's for sure, but she's so good to me. I just don't get it."

That evening, I was in my room doing some homework when I heard Mrs. M talking with someone. I hadn't heard anyone come to the door or the phone ring. I went downstairs to get something to drink and saw Mrs. M in the den, putting food in the fish tank. She wasn't talking to the fish. She was talking to Priscilla, but there was no one else in the room. I stood in the doorway looking straight at her. She continued looking down as if talking to a child.

"I know you love these fish, honey. I would let you feed them, but you always put too much food in the tank. Look, Priscilla, there's your favorite Angel fish!"

I went into the kitchen for some water. Mrs. M had finally allowed me to get drinks for myself. I walked back into the den and said, "Mrs. M, Little Girl is by the back door. I think she needs to go potty. Should I let her out?"

She stopped talking, looked up at me and stared for a moment. Then, as if something clicked in her head, she said, "Oh..., no, I'll let her out." She acted normal for the rest of the evening. We both went to bed at the same time. It was quiet. I listened until I heard her snoring and then I fell asleep. I was so glad Mr. M would be home soon.

The next day in school, I was getting a drink at a water fountain when a girl came up to me and introduced herself.

"Hi, I'm Emma; Emma Chang, and you're Mattie, right?"

I blotted the water from my lips with my hand, "Yes, I'm Mattie Celi. You are new in school?"

"Yes, my family just moved here from the Philippines. My dad just retired from the Air Force. I don't really know anybody. Mr. Sweet recommended that I introduce myself to you. I'm in one of his classes."

Emma Chang had an infectious smile. She said her mom was from the south and her dad was of Chinese heritage. Her hair was a medium brown and feathered around her face. The length was just below her ear lobes. Her eyes were slightly slanted and sincere. She definitely wasn't shy, but I liked her right away, especially since Mr. Sweet sent her my way.

"It's nice to meet you, Emma. Why don't you join me and my friend Joanne for lunch? We usually eat on the picnic tables outside the Crapeteria, I mean, Cafeteria." We laughed.

"Okay, sounds great! See you there," she said as she almost skipped away.

After Emma walked away, I realized I should have asked Joanne first. Oh well, it was done, and I was sure it would be okay. It was. Joanne welcomed her at lunch that day.

Mr. McNeedy arrived as usual on Friday evening. Mrs. M had a nice dinner ready for us. She invited me to eat with them in the kitchen. After dinner I went to my room. I needed to figure out a way to talk to Mr. McNeedy when she wasn't around.

Joanne had invited me to her house for a sleepover on Saturday night. Mrs. M said it was alright as long as they picked me up and brought me back. She spoke with Joanne's mom and confirmed everything. It was so much fun. We ate junk food, watched videos, painted our nails and toes, terrorized her little brother, and played with each other's hair.

"Joanne, what do you think of Emma?"

"I like her. She's easy to talk to, and she has a nice personality. But, we'll have to get to know her a little more before we know for sure if she's okay."

"Right, I agree. She's in my Government class. Mr. Edwin likes her, but then, he likes all the good looking girls."

Mr. Edwin was a flashy dresser. He wore two-toned shoes, bright colored pants and a colorful jacket. His brown hair was slicked back. He wasn't that good looking, but he thought he was. His cologne gagged me.

Joanne's mom had a friend over for breakfast on Sunday morning that owned an Ice Cream and Candy Parlor. Mrs. Gorski offered Joanne and me part time jobs, if we wanted them. We did. I would have to get permission from Mrs. M. I was excited. This was a chance for me to start saving money.

Joanne and her mom dropped me off on Sunday afternoon. Mrs. M invited them in for tea. I told Mrs. M about the job offer. Both parents discussed it and agreed it would be good for us, as long as it didn't interfere with our school work.

On Monday afternoon, Mrs. M signed the permit for me to work. I started working on Tuesday. My schedule was after school on Tuesdays and Thursdays, and all day Saturdays. Joanne's work days were Wednesdays, Fridays and all day on Saturdays. Saturdays were the most fun days because we worked together.

I never had a chance to speak with Mr. M about Mrs. M before he left on Monday morning. I was going to write him a note and somehow slip it to him before he left, but I chickened out at the last minute. I was worried that he would show her the note.

Over the next few weeks, I caught Mrs. M talking to Priscilla several times. It sort of became routine. However, I thought, if she ever wanted me to get in on their conversations, I'd call 911! Thankfully, she started leaving the green door unlocked while she was in there.

Mrs. M drove me to and from work. She helped me open a savings account at her bank and said I could keep some money out for the week. One thing was for sure, she really took care of me. When we were together, she treated me like I was the most important person in her life, except when Mr. M was home. I grew to love her and at the same time, I was sort of scared of her.

Mrs. Outen would come into the ice cream parlor with her two small boys to see me. I kept her informed on what was going on with Mrs. M.

"Honey, I think you're doing the right thing. You'll know when to get help if you need it. She obviously loves you and takes care of you but continue to keep your eyes open."

Joanne and I became close friends with Emma. The three of us ate lunch together almost every day. I finally told Emma that I was in foster care with Mr. and Mrs. McNeedy, and I would appreciate it if she wouldn't tell anyone about my situation. The one thing I didn't tell her about, was how strange Mrs. M was.

Emma said, "I would've never guessed. I would love to hear your story some time."

One Thursday evening, Emma came into the parlor with her older sister, Becky. Becky was a year ahead of us in school. She was petite and had a sweet giggle. Emma invited me to her home for dinner on Sunday. She wanted me to meet her family. I asked Mrs. M when she picked me up from work that evening. She said it was fine as long as they picked me up and brought me home by 9:00PM. I told Emma the next day. Mrs. Chang called Mrs. M to confirm.

I was nervous about meeting Emma's family. What if they didn't like me? I met her dad, Mr. Willy Chang, when he and Emma picked me up that Sunday afternoon. I liked him. He was tall and confident with a warm smile. As we pulled in their driveway, Emma's three younger brothers came running out to greet us.

"Guys, this is Mattie," Emma said. They said hello to me in unison. How cute, I thought!

Mr. Chang said, "This is Adam, Doug and David. Let's go in the house." Once we were inside, Mr. Chang introduced me to Mrs. Chang. I was surprised to hear her southern accent. Her name was Jane.

They lived in a two-story track home. The furniture in the living room and dining room was oriental style black lacquer. It was beautiful and comfortable looking. Emma and her brothers showed me their home while Mrs. Chang finished preparing a Chinese dinner. Little Doug stayed right by my side the whole time I was there and insisted on sitting beside me at the dinner table.

Emma told me she had an older sister, Dana, that was married and lived nearby, but couldn't make it for dinner. Mr. Chang took a picture of all of us standing at the table before we sat down to eat.

Food was passed around and plates were filled.

Mrs. Chang asked, "Mattie, do you need anything?" "Would you pass the butter, please?" I asked. Everyone at the table stopped what they were doing and looked at me. My face got red. Emma started laughing and told me that they didn't use butter on rice, maybe soy sauce? Everyone laughed, and so did I. That was my first Chinese meal, and it was awesome.

Mrs. Chang said, "Mattie, if you want butter, I can get some out of the fridge."

I politely declined. The rest of the evening felt so much more like home to me with all the kids running around. Becky helped her mom with the dishes so Emma and I could visit. I heard all about their travels as a military family. Emma told me she was happy to be back in the States.

I thanked Mr. and Mrs. Chang for a wonderful meal and visit. Mr. Chang and Emma took me back to the McNeedy's right on time.

Mr. and Mrs. M were sitting in the living room talking when I came in.

Mrs. M asked, "How was your dinner with the Changs, Mattie?"

"It was great. Mrs. Chang cooked a Chinese meal. It was the first time I had ever had Chinese food. They all looked at me funny when I asked for butter to put on the rice. Emma said they use soy sauce. It was embarrassing."

Mr. M said goodbye to me because he would be gone in the morning before I got up.

I said goodnight to them and went to my room. I opened the closet to get out an outfit to wear the next day and noticed that the little girl's outfit was gone! I didn't even want to think about that, so I purposely started thinking about my sister and brothers. I wondered where they were and if they were okay. I wondered if my mom was alright. Being at the Chang's made me ache for my family. I was

so happy for Emma. She had a great family.
    I cried myself to sleep, again.

Chapter 13

April 2008 – It was late Tuesday afternoon at the Ice Cream Parlor when two people came in. It was my mom and the old man! I was the only one working that evening so I *had* to serve them. I stood there like a statue, not knowing what to do or say. The old man looked at me and then did a double take. I looked at him and then over at my mom.

"Hi, Mom," I said as I dabbed my sweaty hands and upper lip with a towel. My heart was pounding hard and fast. I wanted to run around the counter and hug her, but I couldn't move.

The old man immediately turned around and stomped out. Mom and I stared at each other a moment. "When did you start working here?" my mom asked nervously.

"A while ago, Mrs. McNeedy signed the permit so I could work and start saving some money," I replied.

"You look good, Mattie," Mom said softly.

"How are you, Mom? And, how are the kids?"

"Everything's fine," she said, ignoring my question about the kids and looking back toward the door. "What days do you work?"

"I work Tuesdays and Thursdays after school and all day Saturdays."

The door flew open and the old man came back in, grabbed my mom by the arm and said, "Let's go."

"No!" Mom said as she jerked her arm out of his hand. "I'll be there in a minute."

The old man grabbed her arm again. I started walking around the counter, "Let go of her or I'll call the police!" He let go and stormed out the door.

"I'd better go. Take care of yourself, Mattie."

"No, Mom, wait! I want to give you my address so you can write me." I ran for a piece of paper and pen, wrote my address down and gave it to her. She shoved it in her purse, turned and scurried out the door. I stood there dumbfounded. My gut started hurting like someone had reached in, grabbed my stomach and squeezed it as hard as they could. I would've thrown up if it weren't for some customers that came in. I collected myself and served them with a half-smile.

I was still in shock when Mrs. M picked me up after work. She knew something was wrong, but patiently waited for me to say something.

"My mom and the old man came into the parlor tonight."

"Oh, boy!" said Mrs. M. "Did he start any trouble?"

"Sort of; as soon as he realized it was me, he turned around and left in a huff. He looked ragged and a lot older. Mom stood there staring at me. She had dark circles under her eyes. She looked worn out. Then the old man came back in and tried to get her to leave. She jerked her arm out of his hand and told him she would be out in a minute. He started to grab her again and I told him I would call the police if he didn't leave. He left. Then she asked me how long I had been working at the parlor. She didn't even give me a hug." I broke down and sobbed all the way back to the house.

"I'm so sorry, Mattie. I'm sure she wanted to, but was as surprised as you were when she saw you. I'm sure she would have given you a huge hug if the old man hadn't been with her. She's probably kicking herself right now for not hugging you." Mrs. M put her arm around me and walked me in to the house. "I'll make us a nice cup of hot tea.

Sit here in the kitchen with me while I make it."

We sat and talked for a while. I told her about the old man and how he abused Mom and us kids. Mrs. M was so sweet and kind. She made me feel better. We ate some macaroni and cheese and watched television until bedtime. I didn't have any homework that night so I decided to write Julie Anne at her college address.

I put a cold, wet washcloth over my eyes so they wouldn't be puffy the next morning. Before I dropped off to sleep, I thought about what happened earlier that day, and what I *should have* said. It's so hard to have words in your heart that you can't say when you want to.

I imagined me making ice cream cones for her and the old man. I would've made a chocolate cone for Mom, chocolate being her favorite, and then a "whatever" cone for him. I imagined putting my thumb in the center of his cone making a big hole. If Mom asked me why I did that, I would reply, "This one's for the asshole."

Mrs. M went to the green room after I went to bed. She kept the door unlocked, but I could hear her talking to Priscilla. I decided I had to tell Mr. M when he came home on Friday night. I couldn't wait any longer.

The next day at lunchtime, I told Joanne and Emma about what happened at the parlor the night before. They were surprised to hear what the old man did, and how he reacted when my mom stood up for me and how sweet Mrs. M was to me when we got home.

"Has Mrs. M done anything weird recently?" asked Joanne.

"Well, she is still spending too much time in the green room, but I did notice the little girl's outfit that was hanging in my closet is gone."

I opened my lunch and found a note that said, "Someone loves you," with a smiley face.

"Oh, she is so sweet!" said Emma.

Joanne jumped in with, "Yes, she can be so nice, but what has she done with the little girl's outfit? I bet it's in the green room. I wish I could see that room, though I'd probably get creeped out."

"No!" I said like a drama queen. "You'd probably slip and fall hitting your head on the corner of a table and pass out. Then Mrs. M would find you and put the little girl's outfit on you while you were out cold. And when you came to, she'd think you were Priscilla and keep you locked up in there!"

While we were laughing, Mr. Edwin, our Government teacher walked by our table and started flirting with us. "I bet that was a good joke I just missed, eh girls?"

Emma played it up with him. "Wow, you sure look spiffy today, Mr. Edwin. Are you going to a party after work?"

I pinched Emma on her thigh under the table and said, "Hey, Mr. Edwin, could you use some help with your work? We're available during study hour. We could help you with your files and maybe grade tests from your other classes for you?"

Just then the school bell rang.

"Come and see me after class this afternoon," Mr. Edwin said, as he winked at all of us and strutted off.

"Yuck, gag me with a bowl of stink bugs," Joanne said. "Don't count me in on your little scheme."

Emma and I ended up working for Mr. Edwin during our study hours. We set up files, graded tests from lower grade classes and typed up various papers for him. We also did something we shouldn't have. We were bad. We sneaked into his cabinet before he locked it up one afternoon and stole the answers to our final Government exam. Emma wrote them down in shorthand. Later, we decided that she would miss two questions on purpose, and I would miss three. What I didn't realize at the time was, it took just as long to memorize that stupid list as it would have taken to review for the test.

After seeing my mom, I was homesick for my brothers and sister. I missed them so much. Louis had a girlfriend he was over the moon about named Kaye, so I didn't see him very often. Every day after school I went to the mailbox to see if there was a letter from my mom or Julie Anne – none.

Mr. M was surprised when I greeted him at the door on Friday evening. Mrs. M *always* greeted him when he came home. He had a perplexed look on his face.

"Where is she? Is everything okay?" He asked.

"Mrs. M is in the green room. She's been acting a little weird lately. She spends a lot of time in there talking to a "Priscilla." Of course, there's really no one there with her. She has called *me* Priscilla a few times. A few nights ago, she woke me up calling me Priscilla and said she just wanted to watch me sleep. It's scaring me, Mr. M, I said, as I helped him with his briefcase.

"Priscilla...she was our daughter that died a few years ago. Are you sure she's talking to Priscilla?"

"Yes, she's been doing this for a long time, but it's getting worse."

"Let's go get her," Mr. M said.

We walked down the hall to the green room. The door was locked. Mr. M put his ear to the door and heard her talking.

Mr. M yelled and knocked on the door, "Sweetie, I'm home. Would you get me something to drink? I'm thirsty."

It got quiet for a moment. Mr. M looked at me as though he didn't know what to do. Mrs. M snapped out of it, opened the door and shut it close behind her. "Oh honey, I'm so sorry, I didn't hear you come in! Go sit in the living room and I'll get you something to drink. Do you want anything, Mattie?"

"No thank you, Mrs. M," I replied. I followed Mr. M into the living room. I excused myself when Mrs. M came back with his drink and went up to my room.

Mrs. M cooked a delicious dinner of pork chops with mushroom gravy, red mashed potatoes and steamed broccoli. She made an apple tart for dessert. I could finally eat a meal and not worry whether my brothers and sister were getting enough to eat. Mrs. Outen had told me not to worry about something you have no control over. It was wasted energy.

"That was an awesome meal, Mrs. M, thank you."

"You're welcome, honey. By the way, you don't have to stay in your room this weekend if you don't want to."

I thanked her and said that I had some homework to do. That was *one* time I was *happy* to stay in my room!

When I went to bed that night, I was glad to hear Mr. and Mrs. M talking and giggling. I went right to sleep. Then, around midnight, I awoke to someone shaking my arm. It was Mrs. M. She was standing over me holding the little girls outfit!

"Get up, Priscilla! Get up and get dressed," Mrs. M said with her eyes glaring at me.

"But, Mrs. M... it's me, Mattie. I'm NOT Priscilla! I'm Mattie," I said half asleep and trying to wake up.

Mrs. M started yelling at me to get up and put the outfit on. I sat on the side of my bed, took the outfit out of her hand and said, "Okay, I will."

Mr. M waddled into the room. "Sweetie, what are you doing? Come back to bed and let Mattie sleep."

"Daddy, Priscilla won't get up and put her outfit on!" Mrs. M was getting more and more upset like never before.

Mr. M started consoling Mrs. M by saying, "Sweetie, it's midnight. I think you might have misread the clock. Let's all go back to bed. She can put the outfit on in the morning, okay?"

Thankfully, it worked. Mrs. M looked at me while I put the outfit at the end of my bed. Mr. M looked back at me and rolled his eyes as he walked her back to their bedroom. I couldn't go back to sleep for a long time wondering what she was going to be like in the morning and hoping she wouldn't get up again that night. She didn't.

I started thinking about what was going to happen to me. Would she be okay or would I have to move again? I realized my body was shaking and my heart was pounding, too. I was so glad Mr. M was home. Mrs. M was good to me, but I was scared. Who am I going to wake up to tomorrow, Mrs. M or...?

Chapter 14

May 2008 – The next morning, Mrs. M scared the crap out of me. She shook my shoulder again to wake me up.

"Mattie, you'd better get ready for work or you'll be late," she said.

It took me a minute to gather my senses. "Oh no, it's 9:00AM!" I jumped out of bed. My head was spinning. Good, I thought, it's Mrs. M.

Mrs. M poured me a bowl of cereal while I got dressed. I ate it quickly and then she drove me to work. It was Saturday. I had to be there at 10:00AM. Joanne was already there. I told her what happened the night before.

"So, you didn't know who you would wake up to this morning, Priscilla's mom or your foster mom, right? That is so freaky. It's getting too serious, Mattie. I think she's going to crack soon and not come back. Then, what will you do?"

"I'm going to call Mrs. Astor and see what she thinks, or, maybe Mrs. Outen. I don't know. I'm hoping Mr. M takes care of the situation, but I don't think he knows what to do."

"I don't know, Mattie. This is serious enough to call Mrs. Astor; my opinion, of course."

It was busy at the store the rest of the day. I was happy to see Mr. *and* Mrs. M come to pick me up after work. Mr. M took us out to dinner that night. Mrs. M acted normal. When we got home, Mr. M had some paperwork to do, so Mrs. M went into the green room for a couple of hours. It gave me a chance to talk to him.

"Mattie, how long has she been like this, and why haven't you told me before now?"

"I'm sorry. I tried to tell you the last time you were home, but you guys were always together."

I proceeded to tell Mr. M about the time I heard her fall in the green room. I went to help her, and she yelled at me to get out and wouldn't let me help her up. I told him about the little girl's outfit and about the night she woke me up, called me Priscilla, and then tucked me in. And, I told him she's been talking to Priscilla in the green room *a lot* lately.

"Remember the night Little Girl was missing? When you two left the house, the door to the green room was open, so I went in. I was shocked at what I saw. There were pictures of older girls wearing the little girl's outfit that Mrs. M has tried to get me to put on, and, one picture of a little girl wearing the same outfit, but it fit her. Mr. M, I think you need to see the green room."

"I never thought much about that room." Mr. M said. "I always thought it was just her craft room. A private space she could call her own. Now, I'm sorry I haven't paid more attention to what she has been up to."

"What are you going to do, Mr. M? I think she needs help. She scares me when she gets into the "Priscilla" mode. What if she doesn't come out of it next time? And, what if it happens when you're not here? What would I do?"

Mrs. M acted normal through the night and made breakfast for us all on Sunday morning. After breakfast, Mr. M asked her if she would go to the drug store and get him something. She wanted him to go with her, but he said he wanted to finish up some paperwork so he could spend the rest of the day with her. So, she gladly went by herself.

"Mattie, do you know where the key is to the green room?" Mr. M asked.

I retrieved it for him, and we both went in. He was shocked to see that it was a "Dark Room" where she developed awful pictures of girls in clothes that were way too small for them.

Mr. M said, "These are pictures of some of the foster kids we've had over the last few years. I had no idea she made them wear Priscilla's clothes. Here is a picture of Priscilla. She loved this outfit and wore it all the time. We had to buy a second one just like it because she wore out the first one. My wife loved her in it as you can see. I don't know what to say, Mattie. I'm sorry you had to go through this. She cares a lot about you and wouldn't hurt you for the world. You know that, don't you?"

"She's been more than good to me. I'm really worried about her."

While she was gone, I called Mrs. Outen. She wasn't home, so I left a message. When Mrs. M returned, I was in my room. She made us all some lunch and then she spent the afternoon with Mr. M. She seemed okay all afternoon, but things changed later that evening.

After dinner, Mrs. M went into the green room and stayed in there for a long time. Mr. M tried to get her to come out, but she wouldn't. He could hear her talking to Priscilla. He called to her several times. Mrs. M finally yelled out to him to leave her alone. She had locked the door and had the key.

"Sweetie, I want some hot tea. Will you make it for me? Let's have some together."

Mr. M could not get her to come out of the green room. He knew he had to do something.

"Mattie, you can go to bed. I'll take care of her. I'm not going anywhere until I get this settled," he said wearily. He usually left early on Monday mornings.

"Mr. M, may I call Mrs. Astor tomorrow? Maybe she knows

where we can get some help."

"That's a good idea. Let me call her early tomorrow. I'll see you in the morning."

I had a hard time concentrating in school the next day. Joanne was home and sick with a cold.

For the first time, Mrs. M didn't make me a lunch. I told Emma at lunch time what had been going on with Mrs. M and what happened over the weekend. Emma automatically opened her lunch container and shared her lunch with me. She was becoming a real pal.

"Wow, it's really getting serious. What are you going to do if she ends up going to a mental hospital?" Emma asked.

"I don't know. Mr. M is going to call Mrs. Astor today to see if she can help. I should know when I get home."

When I got home after school, I thought more about Emma's question. It made me worry more about Mrs. M, and about me, too. I didn't want to move again.

I found a note from Mr. M. "Mattie, I took Mrs. M to the Mental Care Health Facility here in Simi Valley for an evaluation. I'm not sure how long it will take. Please stay home, and take Little Girl out back to do her duty and feed her. I'll be home sometime this evening." Thanks, Frank (Mr. M).

I was worried about Mrs. M. I hoped with all my heart she would be okay and would be able to come home. I sat by the phone wringing my hands. Little Girl stayed right by my side all evening. I think she knew something was wrong.

I jumped when the phone rang. It was Mrs. Outen. I quickly told her what was going on, and said I would call her back because the McNeedy's didn't have call-waiting.

"Okay, honey, I'm sure they'll take good care of her. Do you want me to come over and stay with you?"

"Thank you, but I'm fine. Little Girl is right here beside me, and

Mr. M said he would be home later."

"I'll pray for her, Mattie. I'm sure everything will turn out fine. Chin up – call me when you can," Mrs. Outen said caringly. I always felt better after talking to her.

Mr. M came home late. He looked exhausted.

"They're keeping her overnight. She was really upset that I took her there. They had to give her a sedative to help her calm down and sleep. She'll see a Doctor and a Psychologist tomorrow. I'll be staying home until this whole mess gets taken care of, Mattie. See if you can get a ride to and from work tomorrow evening."

I heated up some leftovers for us to eat. Poor Mr. M was sweating and worried sick. After he ate the leftovers, he wanted more to eat. I made him a sandwich and then gave him some ice cream and cookies. He told me he eats when he's stressed.

Little Girl wanted to sleep on my bed that night. I let her. Mrs. M wouldn't know, and I felt better with her there beside me.

The next day in school, I asked Joanne if she would work for me that night. I told her what was happening. She said she would. I thanked her and told her I was glad she was feeling better.

When I got home from school, Mr. M was there. Mrs. M was still in the hospital. He said, "They want to keep her for a few days so they can do a thorough evaluation. I have to go away for a couple of days. Do you have any friends you could stay with while I'm gone, Mattie? I'll be back on Friday afternoon. It's an important account that I have to take care of."

"I'll call Emma and see if I can stay with her," I said, as I picked up the phone. I asked Emma. She kept me on the phone while she asked her parents if I could stay with them for a couple of nights. Mr. M would be back on Friday afternoon. He would be there when I got home from school.

"They said yes. So, you'll come home with me tomorrow after school?" asked Emma.

"Yes, I'll bring a bag of clothes to school with me. Thank you so much, Emma. And please thank your parents for me."

"We're looking forward to having you. It'll be fun. What will you do with their dog, Mattie?"

"Mr. M is taking Little Girl with him, but thanks. Oh, I forgot, I have to work Thursday night!"

"Oh, no worries, we'll take you to work, and if you don't mind, I'll hang out with you at the parlor," Emma said.

"That will be great! Thanks so much. See you tomorrow."

I told Mr. M I could stay at the Changs, and he was relieved. I went to gather some things to take to Emma's the next day. Mr. M gave me some money to buy lunch at school for the next three days. Then he gave me his cell phone number. I gave him the Chang's phone number, fed the fish and went to bed. Mr. M took care of Little Girl.

Wednesday night after dinner, Emma and I studied for final exams coming up at the end of the month. Being with Emma's younger brothers made me homesick for my brothers and sister. It seemed like it had been forever since I had seen them. I hoped they were okay and that they hadn't forgotten me. I still hadn't received a letter from my mom or Julie Anne.

Emma and I were getting closer as friends. And, her family made me feel so comfortable.

Mrs. Chang said, "You are always welcome to stay with us, Mattie. Please let me know how things turn out for Mrs. McNeedy, will you?"

"Yes, I will, and thank you so much for everything." I loved her slightly southern accent.

It was fun having Emma at the store Thursday night while I worked. She greeted customers and helped me clean up at the end of the night.

Mrs. Gorski, the owner of the Ice Cream and Candy Parlor hired a manager for both of her stores. His name was Keith. Keith was tall, with broad shoulders, green eyes and medium auburn hair in a sort of shaggy cut. He was a big guy, but not fat. Okay, he was gorgeous. He was quiet, but not shy. He was all business and a good manager. I looked forward to seeing him when he came in to the store to do some work. He liked the way Joanne and I handled customers, and that we kept the place clean.

I told Emma, "I think I have a crush on Keith."

Emma instantly replied, "Forget him, Mattie. He's too old for you; he's 22 and your boss! Oh, and don't forget that you're under age, too."

"But, I like older guys. The guys our age are too immature," I replied with a puppy smile.

After school on Friday, I ran home from the bus stop, checked the mail, and ran into the house. Mr. M was home.

"Hi Mr. M, what's happening?" I anxiously asked.

"Hi, Mattie. "Well, there's good news and bad news. The good news is that the doctors think they can make Mrs. M well. The bad news is, it will take a while. They want to keep her for another week or two and then see her as an "out patient." I called and spoke with Mrs. Astor. She's coming by here shortly to talk to us. I picked up some fried chicken and sides at the supermarket for dinner."

"Can I go see Mrs. M?"

"No, I'm afraid not. They won't let anyone see her but me. I'm sorry, Mattie," Mr. M said.

"How is she? Did you see her today?"

"Yes, I saw her this afternoon. She was acting normal, but angry. She wanted to leave the hospital, of course. She asked about you. I told her you were doing great, and you missed her. She said to tell you she'll be home soon."

The doorbell rang. It was Mrs. Astor. I let her in, and she gave me a hug. "Mattie, how are you? You look wonderful," she said.

We went into the living room to sit with Mr. M. I asked if I could get us something to drink, but everyone declined.

Mrs. Astor looked at Mr. M and said, "We have a different kind of problem here, Mr. McNeedy. How is Mrs. McNeedy?"

Mr. M told her all about Mrs. M's status and wanted to know what he should do about me.

"I'll have to be on the road for at least three days out of every week while she's in the hospital. We don't want to lose Mattie. Do you have any suggestions?" Mr. M said nervously. He was wiping his forehead with his handkerchief.

"Under these circumstances, I'm supposed to take Mattie back to Juvenile Hall until things are worked out for her."

I jumped in, "Mrs. Astor, what if I could stay with my best friend and her family for a while?"

I told Mrs. Astor about Emma and her family and that I had stayed with the Changs for a few days this week already, and that Mr. and Mrs. Chang know what's happening. They said I could stay with them whenever I wanted to.

Mrs. Astor replied, "Well, Mattie, if it were anyone but you, I would march you right back to Juvy. However, if you want me to, I'll speak with the Changs. What do you think, Mr. McNeedy?"

"The Changs are a first class family. I think it would be better than taking Mattie out of school during final exams. She'll be graduating soon," Mr. M replied. "How soon could you let us know so I can plan my business trip?"

I looked anxiously at Mrs. Astor as she said, "Why don't I call the Changs right now."

Mrs. Astor and Mr. M talked more about Mrs. M's status before she called the Changs.

"That's very nice of you and Mr. Chang. Shall we agree on two weeks for a start? Mr. McNeedy should know by then what Mrs. McNeedy's status will be. In the meantime, I will be looking for another foster home for Mattie, just in case things don't work out for the McNeedys."

Mrs. Astor said the Changs talked it over while she was on the phone with them. Mrs. Chang said they understood the situation and Mattie was more than welcome to stay with them as long as she needed to.

Mr. M looked at me and said, "Don't worry, Mattie. I'm sure Mrs. M will be coming home soon, and everything will be fine."

"I hope so, Mr. M."

Mrs. Astor had given Mrs. Chang her phone number. She planned to go over and meet the Changs on Monday afternoon. Mr. M would be leaving on Tuesday morning. I walked Mrs. Astor out to her car.

I felt bad for Mrs. Astor. She told me that her case load was off the charts. She worked with a Family Resource Worker to find foster homes for kids in regular and emergency situations. She said that there were over 80,000 foster children in California, and over 80 percent of them suffer some kind of mental health issues. I had wanted to talk with her about my breakdown before I left the Savoys. I then understood why she wouldn't be able to get me an appointment with a Psychologist, because I'd be on a long, long, long list.

Mr. M and I sat and ate the fried chicken dinner he brought home for us. He tried to reassure me that everything would be okay.

I tried to sleep that night, but worried about Mrs. M. And, I did not want to go back to Juvy – no way. I missed Louis, my mom, my brothers, Tony and Matt, and my sister Angie. I wondered, do they miss me, are they angry that I left them, where are they, and how are they? I tried to remember what Angie, Tony and Matt's faces looked like. It had been way too long.

Why hadn't my mom written to me? She obviously didn't care. And what would happen to me if I couldn't stay at the McNeedys? I had the worst stomach ache. I wondered about living with the Changs, but they had a big family and not much room. I had to stop thinking about it. I think I fell asleep out of pure exhaustion.

Chapter 15

*E*nd of May 2008 – I had a feeling the store manager, Keith, liked me.

I thought I tried hard not to let him know I had a crush on him. Joanne didn't think so. "Oh, my God, Mattie, it's written all over you. You stare at him, you giggle when he's around. Come on, get a grip. He's too old for you, anyway."

"That's what Emma told me; am I really acting that stupid?"

Joanne looked at me with her arms crossed in front of her and said, "Yes, end of subject."

When I sat next to Keith going over receipts for the day, I felt tingly. My hands would get cool and sweaty. I made sure I sucked on a mint or chewed gum before I got close to him. He was usually quiet, mysterious, and focused on the business. After what Joanne said, I realized I was acting like a dork. I decided to stop doing all the things that might make him think I liked him.

Staying with the Changs was different for me after the quietness of the McNeedys. It was hectic, but I enjoyed it. The boys were running around, skateboarding, riding their bikes or wrestling with each other. Little Doug especially liked me and would hang on to my ankle while I dragged him around the house. And, it was great doing girly things with Emma and Becky.

Emma and I studied for our final exams. We were A-students. Joanne did well, too. The three of us continued to eat lunch together every day and would continue until we graduated in the first week of June.

It had been almost two weeks and I was getting antsy. I hadn't heard from Mrs. Astor or Mr. M, so I asked Mrs. Chang, "Have you heard from Mrs. Astor?"

"No, but I expect we'll hear from her soon."

That night, Emma asked me a question that took me by surprise.

"Mattie, Becky and I talked with my mom and dad about your situation. We wondered if you would like to come and live with us. Mom and Dad would take the necessary steps to become foster parents. You don't have to answer us right now. Think about it."

"Uh…are you serious?" I asked. I didn't know what else to say. I was surprised.

"Serious as a heart attack," Emma said with a smile. We haven't asked the boys, but I'm sure their answers would be yes."

After sitting in silence for a few moments, I had some questions to ask them. Emma went to get Becky. We closed the door to Emma's bedroom. I sat in a chair and Emma and Becky sat across from me on Emma's bed. Emma said, "Shoot!"

Emma and Becky shared a big rectangular room that had a fan-divider that was pulled across the middle of the room and hooked to the wall on the other side. It made the big room into two smaller rooms. They each had their private space when they wanted it.

"Well, first, you two have your own bedrooms. Where would I sleep?"

Becky responded, "We would push back this divider, put your bed in the middle with a dresser. It would be sort of like a dorm room. That's the way it was before Dana moved out."

I looked at Emma and then at Becky. Tears welled up in my eyes.

"You both would do that for me? You would give up your privacy for me? Are you *sure?*"

Emma smiled and said, "Sure! We keep the divider back most of the time anyway."

Mrs. Chang yelled, "Girls, dinner is almost ready, set the table, please."

The three of us ran downstairs. Emma and Becky set the table while I played tag with the boys.

After dinner, the phone rang. We heard Mrs. Chang say hello to Mrs. Astor. She left the kitchen to talk as she wiped her left hand on her apron. I was anxious to hear what was being said. I rubbed my hands together and paced back and forth.

Mrs. Chang came back into the kitchen and said, "Mattie that was Mrs. Astor. She spoke with Mr. McNeedy. He said that Mrs. McNeedy is doing better and will be coming home next week. I expect you'll be able to go back as soon as she is home. Have you girls had a chance to talk?"

Emma said, "Yes, we talked before we came down for dinner."

Mrs. Chang asked Mr. Chang, the girls, and the boys to come into the living room for a family conference. Wow, I thought, a family conference – how cool!

"Well, Mattie, no pressure, of course. Mr. Chang, myself and the kids have discussed having you come live with us. We would love to have you. I haven't said anything to Mrs. Astor. We wanted to run the idea by you first," Mrs. Chang said.

I didn't know what to say. To live with the Changs would be awesome, but I would feel bad leaving Mrs. McNeedy. She had been so good to me. I had to admit that she scared me when she went into that "Priscilla" mode. Her eyes would bug out behind those thick glasses and she would get angry. It was scary. She probably didn't understand why I couldn't see Priscilla. I thought about pretending I *could* see her and talk to her in front of Mrs. M, but I didn't want to make the situation worse. The more I thought about it, I knew I would be better off not living with Mrs. M. It was too weird. I quickly made my decision.

"Yes, I want to come and live here if you'll have me. But, I have a couple of questions for you."

"Ask away, Mattie," said Mr. Chang.

"Would you let me keep my job at the store? Mrs. M helped me open a bank account so I could save money for a car and maybe an apartment when I turn eighteen. I've been keeping a small amount out of my checks for weekly expenses at school. So far, I've saved a small amount. I still have a long way to go. And, how would I get back and forth to work? Mrs. M took me and picked me up."

Mrs. Chang said, "Yes, of course you should keep your job and your bank account. I think it's great that you're being responsible with your money. We would continue to get you back and forth to work just like we have in the last two weeks. You may occasionally have to take a bus to work, but we would always pick you up after work. How does that sound to you Mattie?"

"It sounds great! I can't thank you enough. You have a wonderful family, and I love being here," I said, trying to hold back the emotion as we all hugged each other.

Little Doug was sitting next to me on the sofa. He grabbed my arm and said, "Oh, goody! You're going to live with us!"

Mrs. Chang interjected, "Well, sweetheart, we'll have to speak to Mrs. Astor and see if we can make this happen."

On Monday afternoon, Mrs. Chang spoke with Mrs. Astor about becoming foster parents and me moving in with them. Mrs. Astor was elated and told Mrs. Chang that she had been diligently trying to find another place for me, but it was hard to place teens in foster homes. She would immediately start the process for the Changs to become my foster parents. Mrs. Chang handed me the phone.

"Hi Mrs. Astor, I'm so happy the Changs want me to live with them."

"I am so happy for you, Mattie. They seem like a nice family. I'm thrilled they will become your new foster parents. I will call Mr. McNeedy and work out a time to take you back on Wednesday afternoon. I'll pick you up after school. I'll be in the faculty parking lot."

"Okay. See you then, Mrs. Astor, and thank you," I replied.

Emma came to work with me on Tuesday night. Keith noticed how much Emma helped out and decided to offer her a job. She had to talk to her parents and would get back with him on Thursday. The weather was getting warmer and business was picking up at a rapid pace. We needed at least two people working during the weekdays now, and three on the weekends. Joanne and I were happy Emma was going to work with us.

I had a hard time going to sleep my last night at the Changs. I was worried. Tomorrow's the big day. I would go back to the McNeedy's. Mrs. M was home. My heart was thumping. What would happen when she saw me? Was she going to be happy to see me, or would she slip back into the Priscilla mode? I decided I would act normal, just like I always had. I wasn't sure if Mrs. Astor had already told Mr. M about me possibly moving to the Changs. I hoped Mrs. M wouldn't get mad at me. I planned on asking Mrs. Astor when she picked me up the next day.

Chapter 16

J

une 2008 – On Wednesday, Mrs. Astor picked me up from school.

"Mrs. Astor, can we go somewhere where we can talk before you take me to the McNeedys?"

"Sure, Mattie, is everything okay?"

"Yeah, sort of, I'm nervous about seeing Mrs. M. I hope she's okay. But that's not what I wanted to talk to you about."

Mrs. Astor looked surprised. She took me to a little hamburger stand where we could sit at an outside table. No one was around. She ordered some iced tea for us. I proceeded to tell her about my feelings of depression and anger toward my mom and the old man. I told her what happened when Mom and the old man came into the store when I was working, and how I threatened to call the cops on him, and how Mom sort of stood up for me. I let her know about my meltdown in front of Julie Anne and Mrs. Savoy the night after meeting Mrs. McNeedy, how I flipped out yelling at them about how weird Mrs. McNeedy was and how I kept saying I wasn't a bad person. And, when I grabbed that delinquent, Marselda by the throat in Juvy, I wanted to continue squeezing her throat until she was history. I was *so* angry, I saw red. It was only when I saw the guards looking at me that I snapped out of it and helped her up off the floor. Thankfully, she was okay, and I didn't get in trouble, but it really scared me that I could get that mad. Then I told her about Rosie and her posse, how they bullied me in school, and the final confrontation at the flagpole.

"Mrs. Astor, I don't ever want to hurt anyone. I mean, I'm never going to become a delinquent or anything, but I never want to see red again, either. It was bad, like looking at a movie through a dark red lens. I think I need some help. Please don't tell the McNeedys or the Changs! I'm really excited about moving in with Emma and her family."

"I'm surprised, Mattie. Why haven't you told me this before now? You're an A-student and well liked in school. I thought you were pretty well-adjusted. Am I wrong?" Mrs. Astor asked.

"No, you're not wrong. I guess I'm a master of adjustment in different situations. It's just…well, when I go to bed at night; I miss my brothers and sister so much. I feel so alone. I never feel like I fit in - anywhere. The holidays are especially bad. All I think about is how I hate my mom for abandoning me and the old man for destroying our family. I don't understand how a mother can choose an abusive alcoholic loser over her children. It hurts. I want to know how I can stop being so angry and depressed. I tried to tell you many times before, but you were always in a hurry - mentioning how overloaded you are with work. They should hire more people to take some of your cases, don't you think?"

Mrs. Astor took a deep breath and grabbed my hand. "I wish it were that easy, Mattie. There is a shortage of funding in this state for foster care. We do the best we can with what we've got. I'm so sorry. It seems like all we do is put out fires. Now, back to you; do these feelings you have only surface when you're alone or in a confrontation with someone?"

"Both, I guess," I said. "You know, I'm worried. I'm going to be eighteen in a year and a half, and it's not that far away. That means I'll be "aging out" into the world and be on my own. I want to be fully prepared, mentally, and in every other way. I'm saving money for that day. I don't want to depend on the Government or anyone else. I'm sorry for babbling on."

"No, please, don't be. I'll see what I can do, okay? It may take a little time. Just remember Mattie, what has happened to you is *not* your fault. I am very proud of how you have handled the changes in your life and that you have a good outlook on your future. I rarely run into a teenager your age that is actually planning for the day they turn eighteen and are suddenly on their own. I believe you're going to be successful, Mattie. You've got what it takes. Now, we've got to get you to the McNeedys. I will let them know about you moving to the Changs when we get there. We'll see how they react – hopefully, okay."

As we pulled into the McNeedy's driveway, I started sweating and my heart was pounding faster than usual. I was looking forward to seeing Mrs. M, but worried about how she would react when she saw me.

Little Girl was barking as Mr. M opened the door. He walked us into the living room. Mrs. M was sitting in a chair staring into space. When she saw me, her eyes brightened. She got up and gave me a big hug. I was so relieved.

"Mattie, my dear, how are you? I've missed you," she said.

"I've missed you, too, Mrs. M."

"Please sit down and have some lemonade, won't you?" Mrs. M said with a smile. She had prepared a tray of drinks for our arrival. I learned a lot about being a good hostess from her.

Mrs. Astor said, "Oh, how lovely, thank you."

Little Girl came to me, and I petted her. Then she went back to lay down by Mrs. M's feet.

Mrs. M had lots of questions for me about how my job was going at the ice cream parlor, how I was doing in school, and she wanted to know when I was graduating.

"I'm graduating one week from today – next Wednesday. I'll be going into the eleventh grade in September," I responded with enthusiasm.

We all talked about the weather and other unimportant stuff. I was surprised Mrs. Astor stayed so long. She finally broke the news.

"Mr. and Mrs. McNeedy, Mattie's friend Emma Chang and her family would like to become Mattie's next foster family. Mr. and Mrs. Chang are in the process of becoming foster parents as we speak.

I personally want to thank you for taking Mattie in and taking such good care of her. From what Mattie has told me, you have been more than wonderful. And Mrs. McNeedy, I'm so happy to see you doing well. I wish you and Mr. McNeedy the very best. If it's okay with you, I will pick Mattie up on Monday after school and help her move to the Changs that evening. I'll keep in touch, and thank you so much for the delicious lemonade," Mrs. Astor said as she prepared to leave.

I looked over at Mrs. M to see what her reaction would be. She didn't say anything. It was almost as if she ignored what Mrs. Astor said. Mr. M looked at his wife with concern.

I walked Mrs. Astor out to her car. She told me she would get some help for me, but for me to be patient, it would take a while. She handed me her business card with her cell phone number on it and said, "Don't give this number to anyone, but call me if you need to, okay? Otherwise, I will be here on Monday afternoon around 4:00PM. Are you excited to move to the Changs?"

"Yes, I wish I could move right now. I hope everything will be okay with Mrs. M."

The rest of the evening was a little awkward. Mrs. M was on medication that made her move slowly. And if she got up too fast from a seated position, she would get dizzy.

Mr. M had locked the green room and kept the key away from

her. She made an easy dinner for all of us, macaroni and cheese and a salad. She actually let me help her make the salad.

The conversation through dinner was mainly me answering questions about the Changs. They liked Emma, but wanted to know more about her parents and siblings.

Mrs. M wouldn't let me help her clean up the kitchen, so I went up to my room after dinner. Mr. and Mrs. M went into the den to watch television for the rest of the evening.

I went downstairs about 9:00PM to say goodnight to them.

"I'm so happy you're home, Mrs. M. See you guys in the morning." They both smiled at me and told me to sleep well.

The next morning, Mrs. M had breakfast ready for us all and handed me a lunch just before I left for the bus stop. I gave her a big hug and said, "Thank you so much, Mrs. M. I've missed you."

Emma, Joanne and I were eating lunch at a table outside the Crapeteria when Rosie the bully walked by, saw me and stopped.

"Hey, how you doin' girlfriend?" Rosie said, checking Emma and Joanne out from head to toe.

"Joanne, Emma, meet Rosie," I said with a smile. They both said hello.

Rosie continued, "Did you hear about Mr. Edwin? He's in jail for taking a fifteen year-old girl to Vegas and trying to marry her. I don't know her name. The authorities haven't released it yet. Yeah, Mr. Zoot-Suit is a real stupid shithead!" Rosie laughed as she moved away. "Hey, if I don't see you before next Wednesday, have a good summer, girlfriend."

I yelled back, "You, too, Rosie!" Joanne and I filled Emma in on how Rosie and her posse bullied me when Wayne was here and how it ended at the flagpole. Emma said, "Darn, I always miss the good stuff, but sorry you had to go through the bullying, *girlfriend!*" We all laughed.

Mrs. M took me to work that night. It was Emma's first day working at the store. I told Mrs. M that Mr. Chang would bring me home after work. It was a really busy night. I was tired when the Changs dropped me off.

Mrs. M had some tea and cookies with me before I went to bed. Mr. M was watching television. He was a couch potato when he was home.

"How was work tonight?" asked Mrs. M.

"It was Emma's first night, and we were really busy. Mrs. Gorski came in and asked us if we would like to work full time this summer. We told her we would let her know on Saturday. Emma's going to ask her parents tonight. I want to because I need to save as much money as I can. I'll be eighteen in less than two years. I'll need a car and an apartment, or a room somewhere. By the way, how are you feeling, Mrs. M?"

"I'm feeling a lot better since I stopped taking that medication they gave me. It was making me tired and dizzy."

"You stopped taking your medication? Does Mr. M know?"

"No, but don't tell him. He worries too much. I'll be fine. I'll discuss it with the doctor when I see him on Monday."

I didn't know what to say. It freaked me out. She's not taking her medication, and Mr. M doesn't know - great. I said goodnight to Mrs. M and walked to the den to say goodnight to Mr. M. On the way down the hall, I noticed the green room was still locked. Good, I thought. Mr. M was asleep in his big chair. I went to bed agonizing over whether I should or shouldn't tell him about her not taking her medication, but then she would get angry with me if I did. I didn't agree with her, I just said goodnight. I was glad Mr. M was home and hoped she would be normal in the morning.

Chapter 17

June 2008 – Around midnight, I awoke to Mrs. M. yelling at Priscilla to get up and get dressed. She was holding the little girl's outfit.

Half asleep, I said, "Oh, no, Mrs. M, it's me, Mattie, *not* Priscilla. My name is Mattie!"

"Don't you talk back to me young lady, now get up and get dressed!" She shoved the little girl's outfit at me. I took it and threw it on the bed. I sat up on the side of the bed and slowly stood up when Mrs. M again yelled at me to get dressed.

"Mrs. M, I'm NOT PRISCILLA!" I yelled back. Mr. M came in the room just as Mrs. M slapped me across the face. Her ring hit the cheek bone under my left eye. He yelled, "Mrs. McNeedy, stop that right now!" He moved quickly and grabbed her arm, pulling her away from me.

I got angry with her and yelled back, "Why did you stop taking your medication? Why?" My face was hot, and I started to cry.

Mr. M said, "You stopped taking your medication?" When did you stop taking it, Sweetheart?" Mrs. M didn't answer. Mr. M turned to me and said, "I'm going to call her doctor right now, and then I want you to get Mrs. Astor on the phone. Will you do that?"

I whimpered, "Yes, of course."

Mr. M took her to their bedroom and called her doctor. I heard

Mr. M tell her doctor what had just happened, that she had stopped taking her medication, and she had slapped me across the face.

"Mattie, the doctor said he would send two people out immediately to pick up Mrs. M. and take her back to the Mental Health Facility."

I called Mrs. Astor on her cell phone. "Hello - Mattie? What's the matter?"

Between sobs, I told Mrs. Astor what happened and handed the phone to Mr. M.

"Hello Mrs. Astor, I'm so sorry to bother you at this time of night, but I need you to come and get Mattie. Under the circumstances, I don't think she can stay here any longer. Mattie doesn't deserve this. My wife's doctor is sending someone to pick her up. I'll be following them to the Mental Health Center."

"I'm sorry, too, Mr. McNeedy. Please tell Mattie that I am on my way to get her," Mrs. Astor said. "Please keep me informed on Mrs. McNeedy's progress, will you?"

Mrs. M had snapped out of her Priscilla mode by the time the mental health representatives came to get her. As they were taking her out to their vehicle, Mrs. M turned and looked at me. She had a confused look on her face. My heart sank to the middle of the earth. I felt like I was losing my best friend.

Mrs. Astor pulled in the driveway immediately after everyone left. We went up to my room so I could pack some things. I showed Mrs. Astor my left cheek where Mrs. M slapped me. It was starting to turn black and blue.

"You can't see it unless I move my hair back. She didn't mean it. Her ring hit my cheek bone. It's kind of sore."

"I know; Mrs. McNeedy wasn't herself," said Mrs. Astor. "I'm glad you called me, Mattie."

"Where are you taking me, Mrs. Astor?"

"I don't want to take you to Juvy because you're going to graduate next week, so I called Mrs. Chang. She was so nice, Mattie. Mrs. Chang said she and Emma would be waiting up for us, and they were glad I called. I am so happy they are available for you."

"Me, too - I can't believe it. Mrs. Outen was right. She told me that if I do the right thing and hang in there, good things will start to happen for me. I feel bad for Mrs. M though, she was really good to me. I'm really going to miss her. I hope they make her better."

I was cold and shaking from nerves when Mrs. Chang opened the door and invited us in. Emma was right there as well. I hadn't known Emma that long, but she was like an angel that came in to my life at just the right time. Emma took me upstairs so we could get some sleep. Mrs. Astor and Mrs. Chang talked for a short time. Becky woke up, said hello, and went back to sleep.

Emma whispered, "I want to hear *all* the details tomorrow, okay? You look frazzled. Let's get some sleep."

I was so tired. As soon as I calmed down, I fell asleep. Then I had that recurring nightmare about me holding a knife over the old man while he slept. I woke up sweating. I told myself I was in a safe place with people that cared about me and *he's not worth one more thought!* I fell into a sound sleep.

While we ate lunch the next day at school, I told Joanne and Emma everything that had happened.

Joanne whispered, "Wow, she really *hit* you?"

"No, she slapped me across the face." I pulled my hair back away from my face to show them mark Mrs. M's ring left on my cheek.

"Are you ever going back to the McNeedys?" asked Joanne.

"Just to get my things and move to Emma's," I said.

Emma, Joanne and I were working on Saturday when Mr. and Mrs. Outen came in with their two little boys to get ice cream cones. I introduced them to Emma. They had already met Joanne. I sat in the corner of the store with the Outens and told them what happened with Mrs. M, and that I was moving to the Changs.

Mrs. Outen said, "Oh, honey, I'm so happy for you. Emma seems like a charming girl. I'll look forward to meeting her family." The store was crowded so they didn't stay long.

On Sunday morning I called Mr. M to see if I could come and get my things.

"Of course, Mattie, I'll be home until 1:00PM. Can you come around 10:00AM? You still have a key, right?" Mr. M asked.

"Yes, I do, we'll see you around 10:00AM."

Mr. Chang and Emma took me to the McNeedys to move my belongings.

I handed Mr. M the little girl's outfit that was still on the bed and suggested to him that he get rid of it before she came home. He agreed and told me he had already cleaned out the green room. The only thing he didn't throw away was pictures of their daughter. I was glad to hear it. I thanked him for everything, gave him the house key, and asked him to tell Mrs. M that I would miss her.

Mr. M handed me an envelope and said, "My wife and I wanted to buy you a new outfit for your graduation. She is very proud of you, Mattie, and so am I. Open it later." I was surprised and gave him a hug. Mr. Chang shook Mr. M's hand, and we headed to my fifth foster home. I watched Mr. M waving at me as we drove down the street.

There goes *another piece of my life*, I thought. I should be happy, but I had a sinking feeling in my stomach. I didn't like leaving under sad circumstances.

Emma and I took the first of my belongings up to the bedroom. I stopped at the door and looked in. The room divider had been pulled back to the wall. There was a single bed with a nightstand in the middle of the room. It *did* look like a dorm room. We put the boxes on my new bed. Emma turned to me and said, "Welcome home, Sis!"

Chapter 18

June 2008 – I opened the envelope that Mr. M gave me from Mrs. M. It was a card congratulating me on graduating from the 10th grade, with a $100 bill, and a note for me to buy a new outfit. I stood there staring at the bill and the note. I missed the McNeedys already.

Mrs. Chang took me and Emma shopping for new outfits to wear on our last day in school. I bought some new tennis shoes, some sandals, a new navy and white dress, and a "Thank You" card to send to the McNeedys. Emma bought some new pumps and a pretty, floral dress. We had invited Becky to go with us, but she was busy with her friends.

Joanne, Emma and I walked around school on our last day having friends and favorite teachers sign our 2007/2008 Yearbooks. Then, we ate lunch together outside the Crapeteria.

Joanne turned to us and said, "I'm going to my grandparent's ranch in Arizona for the summer. I won't see you guys until school starts in September. I already told Keith I quit. I know you and Emma will have a good time this summer. I'm looking forward to being with my grandparents, but also their ranch manager - he's a cutie!"

"Oh, oh," Emma said.

I said, "I'll miss you, but I hope you have a fun summer."

Joanne responded, "I think it is so cool that you are living with the Changs, Mattie! I won't worry about you at all, now."

During the next few weeks, I noticed Keith checking me out as I worked. Sometimes he would stand real close to me, and my heart would start racing. My crush on him was getting worse. I couldn't tell if he knew. It was hard to tell what he was thinking. He was so quiet most of the time. Then, one afternoon while I was in the storage room putting some stock away, Keith came in and closed the door. I stood up. He looked at me.

"Do you need me for something?" I asked as he moved toward me.

"Yes, I do," he said in a soft, sexy tone. He came right up to me, put his arm around my waist, pulled me close to him, and kissed me softly and tenderly. I kissed him back. I wanted time to stand still. But I heard Emma calling me. A crowd of people came in. Keith let go of me and told me to go help the customers. He wiped the lip gloss off of his lips with his hand as he watched me walk out of the storeroom. I couldn't believe what had just happened. I was in a daze.

Emma told me that night, "I know what's going on with you and Keith, Mattie. You *have* to stop it. He could get in serious trouble because you're a minor. You're under eighteen, Mattie."

"But I don't want to. Why does something that is so exciting, have to be so bad?"

"You know why, Mattie. I don't want you to get in trouble, if you know what I mean."

I didn't want to, but I avoided Keith for a few days until one night, he called me at home. Mrs. Chang answered the phone.

"May I speak with Mattie, please," he asked.

"Who may I say is calling?" Mrs. Chang asked.

"This is Keith, the store manager where Mattie and Emma

work."

"Yes, Keith. I know of your interest in Mattie. It is inappropriate. She is a minor, Keith. She's sixteen years old. I will tell you this one time, and one time only; stay away from Mattie. Do you understand me? As of this moment, Emma and Mattie no longer work for you. Please have their checks ready tomorrow. I will personally pick them up from you."

"Yes, Ma'am, I'll have them ready, I didn't mean to cause any trouble."

"Good. See you tomorrow around 5:00PM."

I wasn't surprised that Emma told her mom about me and Keith. Mrs. Chang came up to our bedroom to speak with us. She told us about her conversation with Keith and that we no longer worked there. I was surprised and looked over at Emma. I felt like an idiot. Emma didn't look surprised.

"Mattie, you are not to see or speak with Keith again while you're living in this house. You are a *minor*. He is an *adult*. He should've known better. Understood?" Mrs. Chang said in a very authoritative tone.

"Yes, Mrs. Chang. I'm sorry. I am so embarrassed." I looked over at Emma. "I'm sorry we lost our jobs because of me." I could feel my face flush.

Mrs. Chang continued. "I'll be picking up your paychecks tomorrow. I know how much you've been through Mattie, however, I'm pretty sure you know that what I did was right, and it was for your own good. Both of you have been working hard in school and at the store. What do you think about taking the next month and a half to have some fun? I will give you both a small allowance every week."

Emma asked, "And, what is a *small* allowance?"

"About ten dollars a week, each," Mrs. Chang said.

I looked at Emma, and we both agreed. Both of us already had some money saved, but I didn't want to use mine because it was for an apartment and a car. I still had a long way to go to save what I would need to be on my own.

Mrs. Chang continued, "I'll give you extra if you want to go to the movies or something like that."

I replied, "Great. Thank you so much Mrs. Chang. I'm real sorry about what I did. It won't happen again."

"I believe you, Mattie. We'll speak no more of it, okay?"

When Mrs. Gorski found out about me and Emma not working at her store anymore, she called Mrs. Chang to say how sorry she was that this happened and that she was going to fire Keith. Mrs. Chang didn't want Keith to get fired. He had been super cooperative, so Mrs. Gorski said she would give him another chance, but would pay a lot more attention to what went on in her store. I didn't understand why everyone talked like it was all Keith's fault. I was at fault, too. I was really glad he didn't get fired.

Since I had more time on my hands, I wrote another letter to Julie Anne at college in Santa Barbara, CA. I hope she answers this one. I wondered how she was doing.

Emma and I had fun the rest of the summer. We went ice skating, shopping, to the movies, and more. I played games with Doug and David, the two youngest boys. Doug would hang on to my ankle and let me drag him all over the house. At bedtime, I would try hard not to think about my brothers Tony, Matt, and my sister Angie. It hurt too much.

One afternoon, Mrs. Chang handed me the phone. It was Mrs. Astor.

"Hi Mattie, how are you doing?"

"Great. How are you, Mrs. Astor?"

"I'm fine and busy as ever. Mattie, your mother called me. Your stepfather is in the hospital on his deathbed. She said he is dying of lung cancer and has only a couple of days left to live, if even that. He wants to speak with you. I think your mom needs your support. Of course, it's up to you. I can take you to see them if you want. Mattie... are you there?"

"Uh...yes Mrs. Astor, he's on his deathbed? Why does he want to talk with me?"

"I don't know. Your mom seemed pretty desperate for you to come to the hospital."

"When would you want to take me?" It was all so sudden. I didn't know what to think. I knew that *I* would definitely have something to say to *him*.

"I'll pick you up tomorrow morning at 9:00AM. I've already spoken with Mrs. Chang. Is that okay with you?"

"Yes, of course, thank you."

Mrs. Astor dropped me off at Simi Valley Hospital at 9:30AM. The receptionist told me how to get to the old man's room. I stood at the door and looked at the back of my mother's head and then over at the old man. His eyes were closed. It didn't look like him. I walked quietly and slowly over to Mom; put my bag on the floor. She looked up at me and said softly, "Oh, Mattie, I'm so glad you're here."

It was hard for me to be there and even harder to see my mother so worn out and fragile. My temples started throbbing. There I was, in a hospital room with my mom, looking at the old man on his deathbed with tubes coming out of his body, and I had no feeling for him – none – zip. How freaking sad, I thought. Mom was the *only* person on the planet that would miss him when he was gone. I wanted to run out and not come back, but my mom needed me.

"What is the situation, Mom?"

"He has been sick for a long time with lung cancer, but it took him down fast within the last two months. The doctor says he only has a few hours left. He wanted me to bring you and Louis here so he could speak with you. You are the only one that came."

I walked over to the bed. The old man looked frail at about 85 pounds. He looked like a skeleton with skin on his bones, and he had an oxygen tube in his nostrils. The sucking and hissing sound of the oxygen machine gave me the creeps.

Mom walked over to his bed, leaned down to his ear, and told him that I was there. The old man slowly opened his eyes, looked at Mom and then looked at me. My heart took a leap and started pounding. Okay, this is real. It is not a dream, I told myself. I do not have a knife in my hand, and he can't hurt me or anyone else anymore. I moved back from the bed. He started to talk in sort of a whisper. I couldn't understand what he was saying. Mom told me I would have to lean down closer to his head. What? No, I didn't want to. I looked at her, and she gave me the "puppy-eyed, please" look. I moved closer to the bed again, and leaned down close to his head, "Why did you want to see me?"

The old man tried to talk, but it came out in a whisper, "I want to tell you how sorry I am – I ruined your family. Your mother is a beautiful, wonderful woman, and you are all good kids." He stopped for a minute or so to gain some strength and then continued, "I ruined your family by not providing well for you. I hurt all of you. I'm sorry. I'm asking for your forgiveness."

I straightened up and held on to the side railing of the bed. I was hyperventilating. He wanted me to *instantly* forgive him – unbelievable. I took a deep breath, leaned down and said, "You're scared, aren't you? And, yes, you ruined our family. And Mom did, too, for allowing you to do it. How do I know you really mean what you're saying?" He closed his eyes. Tears slowly bubbled at the outside corners of his eyes and trickled down his temples to his ears. He swallowed a couple of times and then asked for some water. Mom gave it to him. He seemed sincere enough, but how would I know for sure? That was the first time I *ever* heard him say anything nice. He abused all of us; he had no friends, and lost every job he ever had because of his nasty mouth. But, as much as I loathed him, I wanted to believe he was telling me the truth and that he was truly sorry.

Then he started moving his hand up to mine. I pulled my hand away. He continued whispering, "Please tell your brothers and sister that I am sorry. I hope they will forgive me someday." I figured by that statement that they weren't too anxious to forgive him, either.

I noticed his breathing was getting shallower. I leaned down one more time and said, "I forgive you for all the pain and suffering you have inflicted on me and my family. I forgive you, but I will never forget." He slowly closed his eyes and took his last breath. The heart monitor went to a straight line and the monitor alarm went off. Mom started sobbing and saying, "No, no, no!" A flood of nurses and other people came in. It was total chaos.

Over the loud speaker came the Code Blue announcement. The doctor came in, checked his pulse and pronounced him dead. He pulled a sheet up over the old man's head and told Mom he was sorry for her loss. Then he looked at me with a puzzled look. He probably wondered why I had no reaction to what was happening. All I could think of was that it was almost over. Mom went over to the bed and sobbed some more. A nurse came in asking a bunch of questions about what Mom wanted to do with the old man's body.

I snapped at her, "Hey – can you give us a few minutes here? Can't you see she isn't able to talk right now?" The nurse's face turned red as she apologized and left the room. I sat mom down in a chair and let her sob her heart out.

Fortunately, Mrs. Astor came back to check on me. She gave my mom her condolences and asked if there was anything she could do to help us. Mrs. Astor was an awesome lady. She didn't have to, but she stayed while Mom spent a few minutes alone with the old man, and until Mom figured out what she wanted to do. She finally stopped crying and gave Mrs. Astor the name of a funeral home that would pick up the old man and have him cremated. The hospital moved the old man down to their morgue.

"Mrs. Astor, I would like to stay with my mom for a couple of days until she gets through this funeral thing. Is that okay?"

"Sure, I think that's a good idea, Mattie. I'll call Mrs. Chang for you," and then she asked Mom if she was going to be able to drive. Mom assured her she was okay. I wouldn't get my driver's license until I turned seventeen, so I couldn't drive.

Mrs. Chang asked to speak to me on Mrs. Astor's cell phone. "Hi Mattie, this is Mom Chang. Are you okay?" I loved hearing her say, "Mom Chang." Somehow it made me feel truly connected to a family.

"Hi, Mom Chang, I'm fine. Do you mind if I stay a couple of days with my mom to help her through this mess?"

"Of course, honey. If you need our help, just call. We'll be here. Do you have everything you need, clothes and such?"

"Thank you so much," I replied. "I packed a few things to wear, so I'll be okay."

Before Mrs. Astor left, she made sure I was okay and told me to call the Changs when I was ready to be picked up from my mom's house. I agreed and thanked her for her help.

Mom drove carefully back to her house. When we pulled in the driveway, my heart started pounding and my hands were sweating. Then, I realized that he was *gone*, he was *history*. I didn't have to worry about him anymore.

Mom opened the front door.

Chapter 19

*E**nd August 2008* – The house was dark and creepy. I could smell the old man. It was the smell of alcohol and cigars. Mom walked into the kitchen and turned the light on.

"Would you like some hot tea, Mattie?"

"Sure. Do you want me to help you?" I asked, as I looked around the kitchen. It looked exactly the same as when I left over two years before. The white cabinets were worn, the table had the same scratches in it, and the blue and white patterned kitchen curtains were faded. At least, the bloodstain on the wall where Mom's head hit when the old man decked her was cleaned off.

"No, I'll get it," Mom said as she navigated through the kitchen like a maid. She served us tea and we sat there in silence for a few minutes. It was getting late in the evening. I was tired.

Mom looked worn. Her once pretty, dark, curly hair was now salt and pepper and brushed back off her face. She had no makeup on. I longed for the day I would see her with red lipstick on. Then I would know she was recovering from her life with him. Her eyes looked sunken and dark. She sipped her tea and said, "I have a job at the Yarn Store. I sell and teach knitting and crocheting."

"That's great. It's perfect for you, Mom; you're so good at it. Do you think you will sell this house and move into an apartment or condo somewhere?"

"Probably, I can't think about that now, I…don't know," she said as she started crying. I got her some tissues. I went over and put my arms around her.

"There goes a piece of your life, Mom. Now, you have a new life ahead of you." I didn't know what else to say. I didn't want to badmouth the old man anymore. She had heard it all, over and over.

Me, Tony and Matt were in foster homes while Louis was still living at his friend Ken's and preparing to get married to his girlfriend, Kaye. Louis and Kaye had been crazy about each other through their last two years in high school. Whatever made my brother happy made me happy.

I asked Mom where Angie was. She said she was staying overnight at a friend's house. Evidently, Angie never went to foster care. She stayed with Mom the whole time I'd been gone. I hoped the old man hadn't abused her.

"What time is she coming home tomorrow?" I was excited about seeing my sister.

"I have to call her tomorrow afternoon after I take care of business at the funeral home."

I could tell Mom hadn't eaten anything, so I made her eat some toast and drink some water. I watched her as she tried to get the toast down. Been there, done that, I thought to myself.

Mom slept in Angie's room, and I slept on the couch in the living room. Thoughts of all the drama that had gone on in that creepy house went through my mind. Sadly, I couldn't remember any good times. I was also worried about having the recurring dream about the old man. Fortunately, it didn't happen, and never happened again. I woke up several times during the night listening for Mom. She was quiet. I was sure she was totally exhausted. I cried myself to sleep.

I thought about the two men Mom had married, my real father and the old man. They were both abusive alcoholics. Why? I never knew my real father. I remember sitting on the floor in front of Mom, looking up at her black eyes, and hearing her cry after he beat her. Suddenly, I felt sorry for him and the old man. What shallow lives they led and what bad people they were, abusing themselves and everyone around them. They're both gone to another place that's maybe not so good. I was glad I forgave the old man, even if *he* wasn't sincere, *I* was. And then, I forgave my real father.

The one person I hadn't forgiven was my mother. Watching her miserable life made me learn not to be weak and to make better choices in *my* life. I didn't want to turn out like her. I wanted her to tell me she was sorry - and mean it.

The next morning, we had some oatmeal and toast, and then headed for the funeral home. They had prepared the old man's body for cremation. I walked in with Mom. We both looked at him in the casket. It was weird looking at a dead person. He looked like a mannequin – a sick mannequin. I left Mom with him and told her I would be right outside in the lobby. That was the last time I saw the old man. There would be no funeral services, only cremation. It was sad. I said a short prayer for his soul.

The Funeral Director gave me his condolences. I thanked him and asked him when the body would be cremated. He said in a day or two. Well, at least the end was near, I thought.

Mom came out with her head down, moving slowly over to the director's desk. They discussed arrangements and payment. Mom was quiet on the way home. We stopped for a few groceries. She called Angie when we got back to the house. "She'll be home for dinner around 5:00PM."

"Let's cook dinner together, Mom. Okay?"

"Yes, that'll be fine," she replied in a low tone. She didn't want to talk. We watched television until it was time to start dinner. I knew she wasn't up to it, but I was sure it would get her mind off of the old man.

I was getting more excited about seeing my little Angie. Then, the front door opened and Angie walked in. She stopped and looked at me. "Angie!" I said, as I ran over to her. I put my arms around her and said, "I've missed you so much." Angie's arms stayed hanging down the sides of her body. She turned out of my arms and went to her room.

I turned and looked at Mom. "What was *that* all about?" Mom looked at me like she didn't want to talk about it. I was so hurt. My heart fell down to my stomach and churned for a while. "Let's just finish dinner, shall we?" Mom said as she called Angie to the table.

Angie came out of her room to the kitchen, gave Mom a hug, and sat down at the table.

We ate dinner with hardly a sound. It made me think of the last dinner (or non-dinner of only mashed potatoes) I had in this house. It was at the big table in the living room. Angie and the boys were staring at me and Louis with scared looks on their little faces as the old man was yelling obscenities and beating on our mom. Now, the look I get from Angie is one of disgust? I desperately wanted to know what was going on with her, but I was not going to start any drama. If Angie wanted to talk to me, I was there. For Mom's sake, I was quiet.

Angie was cool to me the whole time I was there, so I focused on Mom. I spent a second night on the couch. Neither Angie nor Mom said much to me, so I called Mom Chang and asked her to pick me up. As soon as I saw her pull in the driveway, I grabbed my bag.

I yelled, "Goodbye, Angie!" I heard no response. Then I told Mom goodbye and gave her a hug. "I love you, Mom," I said. "I'd like to see you again. Call me when we can get together, okay?"

She replied, "Okay, be careful."

I ran out the door to Mom Chang's car. I didn't want her to go in that house. It would've been hard on Mom, Angie - and me. I thanked Mom Chang for picking me up. I sat quietly in the car over half the way home. She finally said something.

"Is your mother okay, dear?"

"No, but she will be after a while. She's so broken down right now. She said she got a job and will sell the house to pay the funeral and other bills. The old man left her in debt. She'll probably move into an apartment. My sister Angie is there with her, so she's not alone."

I wanted to cry, but I was still angry. Mom didn't even say I love you or I'll miss you. And, Angie; what happened to her that she was so cold to me? What had they done to her?

Mom Chang made a nice dinner for everyone. There was teasing, laughing, and lots of smiles going on at the Chang dinner table. I loved it. After dinner clean-up, Becky, Emma and I went to our room. I told them everything that happened. The old man was finally gone and gone for good. For me, it was something to celebrate, but I couldn't seem to bring myself to do it. I told them how hurt I was when Angie was so cold toward me.

Emma said, "It sounds like Angie is angry because you left her. Who knows what the old man and your mom have said to her. Once you left and then the boys left, she was alone."

Becky agreed with Emma. It was so wonderful having Emma and Becky there for me.

"I think you're right," I said. "Someday, I hope to square things with Angie; maybe when I'm out on my own."

I called Mrs. Outen to tell her what had happened with the old man dying and me being there for my mom. I didn't mention Angie.

"Honey, your mother has been through a lot in the last few years. I pray for you and your family every day. Thankfully, you and Louis are strong. Things will get better for everyone as time moves forward. Say hello to the Changs for me. They're good people."

Emma and I continued to save money and talked about getting an apartment together. We needed better jobs that would pay more. At dinner one night, Dad Chang told us about some Civil Service jobs that he thought were available. We would have to take the Civil Service exam and pass it with a score of 90 or better to get hired right away. We were on for the challenge. The jobs we looked at were clerical jobs. Dad Chang explained that once we became permanent Government employees, we could apply on other administrative, technical, contracting jobs, and make much more money.

The Government might even put us through school. Dad Chang would take us when we were ready.

We were back in the swing of school in September and back with our friend, Joanne. We had lunch together almost every day. Joanne told us about the summer on her Grandparent's ranch. She had a great time learning how to ride horses.

"And Joanne, what about the ranch manager?" I grinned.

Joanne pouted, "I was bummed. He had a girlfriend."

Emma and I said, "I'm sorry," at the same time.

I turned seventeen in January of 2009. The Changs had a birthday dinner for me. Dad and Mom Chang gave me a cell phone. It was on their family plan so my allowance would cover the monthly costs. Of course, I was warned not to run up the costs by too much texting. I was so happy to have a phone; there was no way I would blow it.

During the summer of 2009, Emma and I got our driver's licenses. Dad Chang had bought a used 1997 Ford Taurus for Becky when she started her senior year in 2008. He bought Emma a 1998 Ford Taurus sedan when we started our senior year in 2009. We had fun cruising around in it and taking it to and from school. Emma and I both took jobs at a large gift shop in town. We worked after school and on weekends. We were getting more excited about moving in to our own apartment together.

I missed my brother, Louis. I saw less and less of him as he was busy with Kaye. They got married after they graduated from High School. I was a bridesmaid in their wedding. My brother was happy, and I was happy for both of them. He started college and worked part time at an appliance repair shop. I knew he was going to do well.

I hadn't heard from my mom since the old man died. I tried not to think about it. I focused on getting ready to be on my own. But, one day I asked Emma if she would drive me to the yarn shop where Mom worked. She stayed in the car while I went in. Mom was busy with a customer, so I waited. She seemed happy to see me. My heart was racing a little.

"You look good, Mom. I want to get together with you." I looked at her expecting a response. She didn't say anything. I raised my eyebrows and said, "Well?"

She finally said, "Why don't you come to my apartment on Sunday after 1:00PM. I get off work at noon."

"Is everything okay, Mom? You're acting a little strange."

"Everything is fine," she whispered back. I wasn't sure what to think.

I agreed, and wrote down her address. She said she had to get back to work. I gave her a hug. She hugged me back. She said she had sold the house, paid the funeral bills and didn't have enough left to pay all the bills the old man had run up. She and Angie were in a one bedroom apartment.

I was always upset after I saw my mother. She made me feel like I was bothering her. It made me even angrier. I chalked it up to her trying to make a new life, but I was determined to find out what her problem was with me. I certainly had a problem with her.

Emma and I stopped to get a hamburger on the way home and talked more about getting an apartment together. We had to get a furnished one and hopefully, a two-bedroom. We started looking around at apartments to see what they were going for. We could afford one if we split the costs.

Dad Chang dropped me off at Mom's apartment at 1:30PM. Emma would come and get me at 4:00PM. I knocked on the door. My hands were cold and sweaty. I was excited, but nervous about seeing Angie again. My heart was aching for her, but I worried about how she would act when she saw me.

Chapter 20

September 2009 – Mom opened the door. "Mattie, come in." I looked around the small apartment for Angie.

"Is Angie here?"

"No, she's babysitting today, would you like some tea, Mattie?" I didn't believe her.

"Yes, that sounds great. Thanks, Mom." Mom looked a lot better than the last time I saw her. She had her hair cut shorter and feathered around her face, and she wore lipstick! She always looked good in red lipstick. She served us tea and some homemade bread she had made. The homemade bread made me think back when Mom and I would make about ten to twelve loaves of fresh bread every Saturday. My little arms would get tired kneading the dough. She would get bags of flour, sugar and canned goods from the local Food Bank.

We made small talk for a while and then I popped an uncomfortable question to her.

"Mom, why was Angie so cold to me the last time I saw her?"

She looked down at her tea and said, "I don't really want to talk about it."

"Well, I do, Mom. Please, tell me. I need to know. I want my sweet Angie back."

"Perhaps she feels you deserted her when she needed you? It's been very hard on her. All of you are gone. She's the only one who stayed with me."

"Oh, I see. You and the old man made her think I deserted her and the boys! Did you explain to Angie that I *had* to leave because of what was going on?" I looked straight into her eyes. She looked down at her tea, again. I continued, "I had no choice, Mom. *I* was being abused, *you* were being abused, we ALL were being abused. Why did you let it happen?" "Mattie, none of this mess would've happened if you and Louis hadn't abandoned your brothers and sister. When your stepfather was released from jail, he became worse and took out his anger on all of us."

"Am I hearing you right, Mom? You are saying it is *entirely* my fault?" Then I yelled, "IT'S *YOUR* FAULT, MOM!" I felt my face getting hot. I looked at her and took a deep breath.

"Mom, I want to hear you say that you knew he was molesting me, that he was getting drunk every night and coming into my room. Thank God he never got farther than fondling me. One night, he said, "Would you have anything to do with me if anything happened to your mother?" I thought he meant he wanted to *kill* you, Mom! I was just fourteen years old! I was scared to death!

Remember the night you came into my room after Angie and I told you what he was doing, and that we were so scared? And the old man told you he was just checking the window to make sure it was locked – really? Mom, ask Angie. She had to pretend she was asleep when he came in."

Mom just stared at her tea. "I never saw him do anything to you."

I could not believe what she said. I wanted to leap over the table and slap her silly.

"Are you *kidding me*, Mom? Of course not; he was sneaking around trying to molest your daughter! Don't you feel responsible for not protecting me? He kicked me in my thigh with his steel toed work boot right in front of you. It left a bruise the size of a football! If Mrs. Outen hadn't advised me to leave, can you imagine what would've happened?"

Mom finally showed some anger and replied, "Mrs. Outen is a child stealer!"

I was shaking all over. I started to realize that she wasn't getting it. She was in some other place, a place called DENIAL. I picked up my tea cup and some spilled in the saucer. My mouth was dry. I wanted this to be over – over for good. But, I was NOT going to leave without hearing her say what I needed to hear and more than hearing it, know that she started taking responsibility for what had happened.

"Thank God for Mrs. Outen. She was NOT a child stealer, Mom. She knew, along with all the neighbors, what was going on in that house. Everyone liked you, but they felt sorry for you and us kids. They didn't understand why you let him abuse all of us. You don't have to be in denial anymore, Mom. He's gone. We need to come to an understanding. I need to hear you say you knew what he was doing, and that you allowed him to abuse us. You didn't protect us or yourself. And you have the *nerve* to blame all this on me, really? You have no idea what I've been through since I left home, Mom. I am finally in a good foster home. The Changs are a wonderful family. But, I've lived in some nightmare situations since leaving. You never tried to contact me or see if I was okay. I have felt totally abandoned by you. It really hit me hard the day of my court hearing. You sat next to the old man in that court room and *lied* to the judge about what happened. Mom, you *let* him abuse us, you gave up your children for him, and you lied for him. Can you even imagine what that has done to all of us?"

I stared at her. We were silent for a minute. I started sobbing. She didn't respond. She just sat there staring into her tea. I felt over-whelmingly alone. The gravity of the moment came down on me like a thousand bullies. I wondered if I would *ever* feel any true love from her. Her light had gone out. I cried for a time until she got up to go get *me* some tissues. I blew my nose and wiped my eyes. A few minutes went by. She lifted her head, looked at me and said, "Yes, I knew what he was doing to you, and I tried to stop him. I understand you had to leave. I'm sorry I let him abuse us. I kept thinking he would change when he got steady work. I'm sorry." She broke down and we cried together. *Finally*, she was taking some responsibility for what had happened.

Angie never came back while I was there. I figured she knew I was coming and stayed away until I left. I asked Mom to tell her I would try to see her again as soon as I could. I decided that the only thing my mom and I could do was start over. It would take some time, but I felt she was worth it.

Emma was right on-time to pick me up. I said goodbye to Mom and gave her a big hug. She hugged me back and said, "I'm sorry, Mattie. I love you."

"I love you, too, Mom. Can we be friends and start over?"

"I think that's a good idea, Mattie. Yes, we can."

When we got home, I told Emma and Mom Chang about the visit with my mom. They were happy about the way it played out. My mom and I were starting over.

I started my senior year looking for an apartment and thinking about a full time job until I could prepare for college. Emma and I had enough credits that we were both going to graduate in January, right after I turned eighteen. After graduation, Joanne was going to live with her grandparents and go to a nearby college. We all vowed to stay in touch.

Emma and I took the Civil Service Exam in Los Angeles and each passed with higher than a score of 90. Soon after, we both had interviews and were hired as clerks at a Government Contracting activity in Los Angeles. We were so happy. We would be starting our new jobs in early February.

Right after Christmas, I found a large one-bedroom apartment that would be available February 1, 2010. Emma and I went to see it. We liked it. The manager was the mother of a girl we went to school with. She said she would hold it if we wanted it. We did.

I told Mom and Dad Chang I would be moving out on February 1st, and Emma told them she wanted to move with me.

Mom Chang said, "Mattie, you're welcome to stay here as long as you like. You don't have to move out right now. And, Emma will not be moving with you if you choose to go. She won't be eighteen until April, and I don't believe she has saved enough money."

Emma was so upset. She tried to talk to her mom, to no avail.

We were shocked. I hadn't thought about Emma not being eighteen until April. Emma was very upset and so was I. Oh crap.

Emma and I graduated early from high school in January with more credits than we needed. We celebrated my eighteenth birthday and our graduation at Disneyland. We had a ball. After we went to bed that night, we both laughed at how we were still virgins! Most of the girls in our school were not.

I had a tough decision to make. I could stay with the Changs, work, pay a little rent, get a car, and maybe even go to college at night. I realized I was fortunate to have this opportunity. But, I was too ready to be on my own.

I called Mrs. Astor and told her I would be moving to my own apartment. She told me how proud of me she was, and that she wished more foster kids would work like I did to be able to take care of themselves when they aged out of foster care. She said there were over 500,000 foster kids in the U.S. It was hard to imagine. I told her about the Chang's offer to let me stay with them, but that I was more than ready to be on my own.

I moved into my first place on the 1st of February, 2010. Dad and Mom Chang helped me move. Emma was too upset. I didn't have enough money for a car because Emma didn't move in with me. So, I rode to work with Emma until I had enough money to buy a used car. When I got a car, I invited my mom and Angie over to my place. I hoped to work things out with Angie.

After I was all moved in and the Changs left, I sat on my couch, holding the key to *my* apartment. I did it! I finally did it. I felt a little panicky - and alone, but in a strange way, I was okay with it.

I never heard from Julie Anne, though I wasn't too surprised. Also, I never received any Mental Health therapy through the foster system. I was okay with that, too. I realized that my anger waned after forgiving the old man, my real father, and most of all, my mother.

My phone rang. Mrs. Chang invited me to dinner on Sunday. I accepted. It was a perfect start to a *new piece of my life!*

CPSIA information can be obtained
at www.ICGtesting.com
Printed in the USA
FSOW01n0219210116
15969FS